ANYTHING SHORT
OF MURDER

Tony Piazza

Revised 3rd Edition

ISBN: 13: 9781519208927
ISBN: 10: 1519208928

This book is a work of fiction. Places, events, and situations in this
book are purely fictional and any resemblance to actual persons,
living or dead, is coincidental.
Printed in the United States of America

Library of Congress Control Number: 2014914387

CreateSpace Independent Publishing Platform
North Charleston, South Carolina

Printed in the United States of America

Editors: Sue McGinty and Marie Marcy
Cover Graphic Artist: Liam Heckman
Author photo courtesy of Charlotte Alexander

ACCLAIM FOR TONY PIAZZA

The narrative (of *A Murder Amongst Angels*) aims for the minimalist prose of Raymond Chandler...More concerned with nostalgia than invention, the plot hits the right notes as it crescendos toward a well-orchestrated coda. A sentimental caper that mostly follows the genre formula, with a few refreshingly original flourishes."

– *Kirkus Reviews*

"In this delightful romp in the classic noir genre, Tony Piazza has captured the glamour and allure of the 'hard-boiled detective with a heart of gold.' There are twists and turns galore in this imaginative tale that in places will leave you breathless." [*Anything Short of Murder*]

– Susan Tuttle
Author of Piece by Piece

"One-time San Francisco actor turned novelist Tony Piazza has resurrected the concept of the ludicrous but exciting adventure yarn with *The Curse of the Crimson Dragon*. Enjoy living in the literature of yesteryear? Then you'll savor leaping headfirst into these pulpish pages. The flowing action and excitement never let up, even during the expository or exotic love scenes, as Ryan faces down every kind of life-threatening situation. The sweat never stops pouring out of Piazza's prose.

If only more writers reminded us of how much fun reading was in the days of *Planet Stories*, *Argosy*, *Fantastic Adventures*, and *Blue Book*!"

– John Stanley
Author of The Gang That Shot Up Hollywood

Old-fashioned adventure and thrills with clearly defined good guys and bad guys, a throwback to another era. I've read both of Piazza's novels and each takes me back to a time and place where I enjoyed spending time."

–Dave Congalton
Radio talk show host, screenwriter, and author

"It's almost impossible to set *Anything Short of Murder* down once I start reading. I have a special love for Tony Piazza's breathtaking characters. I feel their personalities jump right out from the pages and into my mind's eye where they dazzle and spellbind me from beginning to end."

– Cookie Curci
Freelance journalist

FOREWORD

nything Short of Murder wasn't originally envisioned as a novel, but got its humble beginnings on a classic movie site under the title REEL MURDER. It was conceived as a serial mystery blog that would take its readers through a labyrinth of clues, mysteries, and cliff-ending situations much akin to the early radio tradition of storytelling. However as this project developed, other comparisons by its fans were also made. Some compared it to Hollywood film noir, others to the writings of Chandler or Hammett, and still others to the pulp classics of the 1930's and 1940's. Whatever the case, it was this type of feedback that encouraged me to expand and polish its rudimentary structure and develop it into the novel that you are holding in your hands today.

I owe a debt of gratitude to all those loyal TCM fans who encouraged me along the way. Especially,

Phyllis Rizzi, Dave Watson, Marie Marcy, and Cheryl McCullah. Without them this book would never have been written.

I also would like to thank my other friends and family for their input, particularly: Al Quaglino, whose vast knowledge in just about everything, but especially firearms, was so helpful. To my sister-in-law, Kathleen Fahmy, who spent time reading and critiquing various aspects of the story, and finally to my loving wife, Susan, for her knowledge of L.A. and its colorful history. Not only was she born and raised in Los Angeles, but she was also able to provide me with a unique perspective, having descended from a family which can be traced back to the original settlers of the city. I therefore had at my fingertips a wealth of information that would otherwise had been difficult to obtain.

I would also like to thank Sue McGinty, who not only is a good friend, but also such a support when it comes to my writing. Her editing skills are par none, and being a marvelous mystery writer herself, I cannot think of another more qualified to help revise this 3rd edition. Of course, any errors that do survive, are once again, mine and mine alone.

Last, but definitely not least, there are three other special people I would like to thank, all of which I know are looking down from heaven. My father, who gave me the opportunities to be able to accomplish my heart's desires; my mother, who taught me the love of literature; and the Almighty, who bestowed upon me the gifts of patience, and sense of right that has seen me through both good and bad times in my life.

Tony Piazza
July 2015

1

A MESSAGE FROM A KILLER

In 1930, Los Angeles was a land of sunshine, tall majestic palms, and golden beaches. A city surrounded by acres of bountiful groves of sweet, juicy oranges, picturesque adobes, and historic old missions.

Los Angeles, whose humble beginnings as a small pueblo in an area known as Olivera Street, presently has grown to a population of 1,238,048. During those early days its inhabitants, the people of Mexico and Spain, produced food, wine, and children. While today, aside from crates of oranges, the Angelenos most lucrative business is creating moving pictures.

As most of the country struggles to survive an economic depression, one of its towns, Hollywood, seems immune to this reversal of

1

fortune. That's because of its product—motion pictures. A person laboring a week for a loaf of bread will somehow find a way to gather up their two bits and slap it down at the box office. Because to them, this ticket is magic; it buys them freedom, if only for an afternoon, from the struggles of the outside world: the country caught up in poverty and in the shackles of prohibition. With this admission price they're guaranteed access into a world that could only be conjured up through the magic of film. A world with dramas, comedies, and westerns as its staples; and musicals like those of Busby Berkeley, whose films are populated by extravagant sets; catchy, uplifting tunes; breathless choreography; and lots of beautiful dames. These diversions have made this motion picture experience like a little taste of heaven for those otherwise in hell.

Hollywood, sometimes referred to as "America's film capital," seems in itself the place of dreams; but the truth however, is vastly different. Just like its images on the screen, those impressions are merely phantoms. The real Hollywood is not so much glamour, but the dross that comes off of it. Peel away all the tinsel and glitter and what do you find: greed, vice, sin, and sometimes murder. That's where I come in.

I was getting a quick bite at one of those high profile delis on Hollywood boulevard; you know, one
of those places reputed to cater to the stars. Of
course, the only star I ever saw go into this joint was
usually attached to the uniform of a beat cop. Anyhow,
I was biting into my pastrami, sitting in my usual spot
at the counter, when a rather slinky blonde cozies up to
my side and whispers something rather encouraging in
my ear. It isn't what you think, but something equally
tempting; she offered me fifty dollars in cash. A com-
modity I've recently been short of. I responded, "Lady,
if it's anything short of murder, I might be interested."

"Funny you should say murder," she responded,
perhaps a little over melodramatically. "Because I believe someone out there wants to kill me."

"Why'd you pick me out of the crowd?" I asked with
sudden curiosity, "And how'd you know that I might be
able to help you?"

"Easy," she answered shortly. "I work for Champion
Studios. About six months ago you did a job for one
of my friends there. A Don Taylor. He's first assistant
on a picture I'm working on. Well, he put me onto
you."

Don Taylor was one of my more successful cases,
and I guess I should've mentioned it earlier, but I am
a gumshoe. Private eye to the more sophisticated; my
name is Tom Logan and I hang my sign over a door just
down the street in a commercial building located on
the corner of Hollywood and Gower. Now, regarding

Taylor; he'd money and a solid job— the perfect in-gredients for blackmail. People were hurting from the previous year's crash, and so 1930 saw a whole lot of milking schemes arise out of the sheer need for easy money. In Taylor's case it was the old badger game, and it nearly worked, except (I say modestly) for my intervention. However, that's now history, and the fifty bucks promised for this job had me looking more fa-vorably toward the future.

I told her that it would be better to conduct our business in a place a little less public, and so having the remains of my sandwich bagged, we made our way down the street to my office.

As we walked, I had a better chance to size her up. The dame was definitely a looker, and her charms did not go unnoticed by most of the males we passed as we covered the several blocks to the art deco building that housed my business. The elevator operator took us up to the fifth floor, and gave me a knowing grin as he held the cage door open for her.

"Keep your mind out of the gutter, Nick. She's just a client," I whispered as I passed by him.

I was still in the minor leagues, so I didn't have a receptionist. It took all the capital I had just to pay for the rental, and it was pretty basic; just four walls, a desk, two chairs, and a couple of filing cabinets.

"Now tell me," I began, once she got seated, "what's this about murder?"

She reached into her handbag and pulled out a neatly folded piece of paper.

"*This* is what I'm talking about," she replied handing it to me.

I walked around my desk and carefully unfolded the note as I dropped into my chair. It was a single page of rather heavy crème colored paper with the words and letters cut neatly from another source and pasted carefully to form the message, "KEep Your mouth ShuT Or DiE!"

"They're from our shooting script," she offered.

I must've looked puzzled, because she quickly explained, "I work as a script supervisor for the studio. Our most recent production is called "KEYS TO ADVENTURE." Those eight letters... K, E, Y, S, T, O, D, and E were cut from the cover. The others I'm sure were removed directly from the script's pages."

"Do you have any idea what it's referring to?" I asked. "Or to what it is that you're to keep quiet about?"

"Not the slightest," she responded, a frown slightly furrowing her brow.

"How was it delivered? Was there an envelope?"

"No. I believe someone must've slipped it into my handbag when I wasn't looking."

"Any suspicions who?"

She shook her head.

"When did you discover it?"

"Two days ago, just after lunch. We were having a meeting in the production room, and half way through I'd remembered leaving my bag in the outer office. After collecting it I checked for my wallet and was surprised to find the note tucked in one of the side pockets."

"Could it have been placed there earlier?" I offered. "Perhaps some time when you'd left it unattended?"

"No, it couldn't have been," she answered without hesitation. "Up to that point the bag had never left my side. And I know there wasn't a note in it earlier that morning."

"Then it's safe to assume that whoever placed it in there must've been associated with the studio," I reasoned. "Did you notice anyone outside of the ordinary hanging around?"

She shook her head again. "Aside from the staff, no. But I'm sure it wasn't any of them. We were pretty much together the whole time. No," she concluded, "it had to be someone who wandered in from the outside… someone with permission to be on the studio property."

"And who have you told about the note?"

"Just Taylor," she answered simply. "At first I didn't take it seriously. I just thought it was a joke. But when I started feeling uneasy about it, I confided in him, and he suggested you."

I switched on my desk lamp and held the sheet up close to the light.

"Heavy weight paper… quality watermark…" I rattled off, noting the details. "Must have come from some expensive stationary," I reasoned. "Whoever composed this note has some dough."

She seemed impressed with my Sherlock routine, and quite frankly I enjoyed putting on the show. "OK," I said, quickly making my mind up, "I'll look into it. Can you get me into the studio tomorrow?"

"Sure," she replied. "I can get you a pass. Just check in at the front gate."

"Tell them I'm a relative. You know, I could be your long lost Cousin Eli or something. Make it known around the studio also. No use arousing more suspicion than we need to." It then dawned on me that I hadn't gotten her name. "Who should I ask for when I call?"

"Oh, I'm sorry; I didn't introduce myself, did I?" She held out her hand. "I'm Madeline Hyland, but my friends call me Mattie."

"Not related to the 'Hyland' of Hyland Dairies are you?"

Hyland milk products were a big outfit in the Southland and my statement was made in jest; that's why it almost floored me when she answered that she was. Her daddy owned the company! Well that explained the fifty in cash. I didn't think a script supervisor's salary would allow the lady to be as easy with her dough as she seemed to be. And speaking of fees, I told her that it would be twenty-five up front and

twenty-five when I've completed my task, plus any additional charges for expenses. These I would submit as
an account at the end. In which she instantly agreed,
placing two bills squarely on my blotter and then running her palm over each as if she were trying to remove
the wrinkles from both Mr. Lincoln's and Mr. Jackson's
jackets.

"See you tomorrow then," I said dismissively, making a show of fumbling through some mail I had earlier dumped on my desk. When I sensed that she hadn't
made a motion for the door, I glanced up quickly. She
was still sitting there primly, her body erect, purse
squarely in her lap, and one long, shapely leg crossed
over the other.

"I have a favor to ask," she started somewhat hesi-
tantly. "I think someone is following me. Could you
please see me safely into a cab?"

"Sure," I said after the briefest of pauses, and then
grabbing my hat from the rack near the door we headed for the lobby.

I'd convinced myself that it was nothing more than
nerves that gave Miss Hyland the impression that she
was being tailed. And who could blame her; getting
a note like she did would give anybody the jitters. At
least that was my conclusion when we had ridden down
on the elevator. However, it was only after I had made
a quick inspection of the street as we were walking toward the cab stand that I realized her suspicions may've
been well founded. Immediately I spotted a dark sedan

parked directly across from the building's entrance, and a man sitting in the driver's seat who was staring none too discreetly in our direction. His window was down, and although he didn't seem overly concerned about being seen, he was taking every precaution not to be identified. For one thing he was wearing a dark gray coat much too heavy for the eighty-degree Los Angeles weather, and a bright red scarf which had less to do about keeping his neck warm than for the purpose of obscuring the lower portion of his face; while a large pair of sunglasses succeeded in concealing the rest. To complete the disguise he had placed a tan fedora low on his brow with the brim almost touching the bridge of his nose. What puzzled me, however, was as careful as he was to hide his appearance, he didn't seem as concerned regarding his presence. In fact I felt that he was going out of his way to be noticed, for it was only after I started to make a move in his direction that he decided to hightail it out of there, pulling a "Barney Oldfield," and guiding his car into traffic, heading down the boulevard… much too fast for me to catch even a glimpse of the car's plates.

2

AN UNSCRIPTED DEATH

"I've been a loner most of my life… although not by choice. It seems like anyone who ever gets close to me usually ends up hurt or worse, dead. While most guys walk arm-in-arm with a girl on a Friday night, I'm more likely to be lying in a damp alleyway with a shiv in my side. I can't afford relationships; they could be deadly for the both of us. It's probably the business I'm in. I walk the streets of Hollywood… not the town painted by myth, but the real Hollywood plagued by drugs, booze, blackmail, and murder!"

I arrived at the studio gates around ten the following morning, announcing to the guard that I had an appointment with Miss Hyland. He waved me through after checking his clipboard and instructing that she could be found on the European backlot. He gave some brief directions that would first take me past a series of sound stages and workshops before leading to some forty acres dedicated to the outside sets…. streets representing various cities in America and Europe; a river with an Amazonian jungle along its bank; a wild west town; and even several buildings straight from ancient Rome or Greece.

As a rule, Champion Studios didn't produce "A" pictures like Warner or Fox; nor "B" for that matter. "Flying C Pictures" usually ended up as a second bill, ("Scratch Features" in movie picture lingo), showcasing its features at a few remote spots of middle America. Serials were their specialty, and some animal or musical shorts.

"Keys to Adventure" was an exception however. A highly respected, "well heeled" producer felt it showed promise and decided to put some real dough into its production. It was no "All Quiet on the Western Front," but as a war picture goes, judged by the amount of action evident on the set, pretty impressive. There were a large number of burnt-out buildings (actually, facades) with fire and smoke courtesy of the special effects department pouring (on cue) out of various doors and windows. 'Extras' in military uniforms, along with stuntmen, ran to and fro to their marks carrying various guns; simulating the type of chaos one expected to find on the battlefield. Explosions also filled the landscape, carefully planted charges that were safely detonated in a sequence dictated by the stunt coordinator.

It was all very interesting, but I had to remind my-self that I wasn't there as a tourist.

As I drew closer I heard the director shout, "cut," megaphone in hand, and then turn to his first assis-tant, perhaps to discuss the 'take.' After a short confer-ence he turned back to the set and bellowed, "I need everyone in their first positions!"

Besides the camera, which was enormous and en-cased in some sort of covering to reduce noise, there were also large arc lights powered by a nearby gen-erator truck, reflectors, and various pieces of sound equipment, including a booth with a Western Electric recording device and a long boom microphone.

Various crew members, some working, some watch-ing with arms folded, lined the edge of the set; these included the director, assistant directors, script super-visor, make-up man, hairdressers, wardrobe, and ac-tors, some of which had their own chairs assigned. It was here that I searched out my client, who wasn't that difficult to find because of her short blonde hair that was now glistening under the intensity of the lights.

I had just taken a few steps in her direction when I heard the director shout, "action!" and the set came alive with explosions, gunshots, and cries from the ad-vancing infantry. At that same instance, a shrill scream issued just to the left of me, but hadn't immediately caught my attention due to all the noise playing out on the set. Filming instantly came to a halt, and what I saw next played out in what seemed like slow motion.

Standing near the chair where Miss Hyland was seated, stood a young woman, hand to mouth, and obviously in shock staring down at my client who had suddenly slumped forward from her sitting position and then pitched head first onto the floor.

I reached the spot in a matter of seconds, noting instantly a small wound to the back of her head. I immediately lifted her fragile wrist and checked for a pulse and then did the same again at the artery in her neck. Finding none, I solemnly announced to the gathering crowd that she was dead.

"She's been shot!" I said, as silently I cursed under my breath. "Someone, call the police."

As a person rushed off to locate a phone, I made a quick examination of the body, making sure not to disturb what could eventually prove to be evidence. The corpse was face down, and positioned like some broken doll, arms and legs bent at odd angles. Leaning low, I brought my face close to the floor trying to get a better look at the wounds, and perhaps draw some conclusion as to the angle of the bullet's trajectory. It was then, and to my surprise, that I realized that the face and blank, lifeless eyes that looked back at me did not belong to the same dame that had been in my office some fourteen hours earlier!

I turned as I heard a sudden gasp from behind and found to my relief, Miss Hyland standing over me, her pale blue eyes wide as China saucers.

"My God!" she cried. "She's dead!"

"Somebody look after her!" I ordered rising quickly. She and the younger dame I had noticed earlier were both staring with a strange, empty, transfixed gaze toward the lifeless body who only moments before had been a co-worker and perhaps a close friend. Recognizing the first signs of shock, I took each gently by a shoulder and turned them away from the sight. I called again for assistance and this time somebody responded: a third woman, who quickly stepped in and with military-like efficiency took charge.

Her nurturing manner was instantly evident as I watched her gently guide them aside, and then speaking in a low, soothing tone, escorted them a safe distance away toward a corner of the lot.

When they were out of earshot, I asked a nearby crew member, "Who was that?"

"That's the hairdresser, Fran Adams," he answered matter-of-factly. "She'll take care of them."

Now, when I'd examined the wounds earlier I concluded that the shot had come from behind, and since I'd observed that there were no powder burns evident on her skin or clothing, this ruled out the killer being in close proximity of the victim. Therefore the shot had to come from a distance. Following this reasoning, I examined the area directly behind me, searching out any corner that a person could be concealed from view, yet be within a straight visual line to the victim. The only location that I could find that would fulfill both those requirements was a number of prop boxes standing about twenty feet to the right of where I was standing. I took a couple of steps in that direction when I was intercepted by a tall, burly man.

"Can I help you?" he asked.

"Not really," I replied. "…just wanted to take a look at those prop boxes."

I tried to push by him, but his large frame blocked my way.

"I probably can help you. That's my department. I'm 'Prop Master'." He put out his massive hand. "Dick Soames."

We shook. He had a paralyzing grip and it took several minutes to get the blood flowing in my hand.

The boxes stood about four feet in height and had the words "Prop. Dept." stenciled in white letters on all four sides. There were six of them sitting beside each other in a row. I asked him what they stored and he told me that they were for the rifles being used on the set.

"What about the pistols?" I asked. "Where are you keeping them?"

He showed me over to a large makeshift bench in the same area which had several rows of vintage World War I guns spread across its surface. There were also a variety of items for maintenance of the weapons lying alongside; most notably cloths, cleaning rods, brushes, oil and lubricants.

"These work?" There were numerous types of armaments: ten 9mm German Lugers, a dozen or so British Webleys, five Colt .45-inch automatics, and a number of revolvers of either Colt or Smith and Wesson manufacture.

"A few have the firing pins removed… most are usable." He pointed over to some medium-sized boxes. "We load them with these blanks."

Great, I thought to myself, a complete armory conveniently set out for the killer's choosing. Slip a live bullet into the barrel and you got your perfect murder weapon; difficult to trace because it is the property of the studio. Chance of discovery: nil, because there's no need to carry it to or away from the crime scene. Not obvious; because it wouldn't seem out of place buried amongst all the other weapons in the prop department.

"Have any of these particular weapons been fired for the picture?"

"Not today," he replied, and then quickly added, "I just laid these out as backup. Sometimes the ones on the set jam, or I'm faced with equipping more 'extras' than the call sheet had originally listed."

"How many of your guns are actually being used on the set at the moment?"

He thought for a second, and then answered, "Thirty that actually fire… another five without firing pins… and fifteen dummy guns made of rubber."

"Number of rifles compared to pistols?"

"There were more rifles than pistols." Again he paused as he mentally calculated the numbers. "I'd say thirty-five rifles and fifteen pistols."

"How many rifles on the set had firing pins… and how many of the pistols?"

"There's about five pistols," he answered without hesitation, "and twenty-five rifles. The director was trying to create his vision of an infantry advance, and requested more live rifles than pistols to play a part. He thought it would look more effective… muzzle flashes… smoke…"

I wasn't there to discuss moving pictures, so interrupted him with the observation, "It seems you keep pretty good track of your weapons."

"I have to. You wouldn't want them to get into the wrong hands…" This last sentence trailed off as the irony of his last statement suddenly struck him.

A long awkward pause followed, and I decided to change gears and try another line of questioning.

"Where were you when the murder occurred?"

"I was over by the sound booth," he answered firmly.

"Did you notice anything out of the ordinary?"

He shook his head. "I was focused on the set."

"And what about, just after the murder?"

He shook his head again, but this time with noticeable hesitation.

"Then, there's not a ghost of a chance that you saw anything strange or out of place?" I asked, gently prodding.

He stopped, considered a second more and then responded thoughtfully, "Well, now that you mention it, I did see a guy run away from the scene just shortly after the commotion broke out. He really hightailed it out of here, like he was running away from something."

"Can you give me a description?"

"Yeah, I think so... about your height... maybe slightly shorter, heavy wool coat... dark color... perhaps black or gray... tan hat and a scarf... I remember the scarf."

"What color?" I asked quickly.

"You couldn't miss it. It was bright red," he replied. "Strange fellow. He's been hanging around the studio for the last few days... on the edge of the set...not talking to anyone. None of us are really sure who he might be, although we all have our theories."

3

A PLEA FOR HELP

*Most times life can be like a game of chance;
you roll the dice and it either comes up eleven
or snake eyes. For one dame, it was both
aces... and she had to cash her chips in early.
I'm like the pit boss... My job is to see who
loaded her dice.*

I left the prop master with very specific instructions. I told him to check the weapons on the bench, and to particularly look for signs that one of the guns may have been recently fired. Heat from the barrel or the telltale odor of cordite would be a good indication. I told him to be cautious when handling them and showed him briefly how to use a pencil in the barrel and a handkerchief so as not to disturb any possible prints left by the killer. I honestly didn't expect that we would find anything that we could trace. Besides the guns having been handled by a great many already, it was more than likely the killer used gloves, or wiped it clean after committing the crime. But, for procedure sake, I decided that we should still play it by the numbers and not leave anything to chance.

As I returned to the body, I noted that the Los Angeles Police Department had finally made their appearance. In the course of my investigations I never really butted heads with any of their officials, at least lately. I think they tolerated me because I used to be one of their numbers, a member of the brotherhood so to speak. Still one could never be sure, so I approached the knot of police officials gathered on the set with caution and a hint of resolve.

"Thomas!" I heard called out in a familiar Irish brogue. "You're nat gumshoeing on this one are ya?"

Sean "Red" Clancy was a shoestring of a man, but don't let appearances fool you. Just over six foot and some 160 pounds, all of which is muscle, he could hog tie the best of them. He carried an air like that of a mischievous child, perhaps created by the flaming red hair which he wore close cropped, and the generous freckles spread across his gaunt features. We had both walked the beat together some five years ago, and had to deal with some pretty nasty characters. He was a good man to have at your back. It had been at least a couple of years since I saw him last.

"How's the force been treating you, Red?" I asked, firmly taking his hand. "I see you've been promoted to detective."

"It should 'ave had been you, me boy! They didn't treat ya so nicely!"

He was referring to my less than honorable discharge from the force. I really hadn't done anything that justified the severity of the punishment. At most a reprimand would have been sufficient.

A bootlegger thought he could buy me, but my fist told him otherwise. Normally that would have been a misdemeanor, but he had a well-placed friend, politician actually, who owned a piece of the business. He pressured my superiors, who eventually sent me packing.

I told Red everything I knew so far about the situation, and we agreed to work "unofficially" together. He called over our only witness, or at least the only one close enough to the victim who could be of some possible help to us. She seemed a lot more composed now than when she had been taken aside by the hairdresser.

"Could ya please state yar name?" Red asked pulling out his notebook.

"Betty Jean Williams," she answered meekly. "Although I just use Betty Jean for my professional name."

She couldn't have been any older than eighteen, about five feet in height, and skinny as a rail. Her skin was pale, almost white, and made all the more evident when contrasted to her large dark eyes and long, heavy black hair. Overall she gave me the impression of a fragile porcelain doll.

"And where do ya reside?" Red asked taking notes.

"It's an apartment complex called the 'Casa de Flores' on North Highland Avenue just off Hollywood Boulevard. I'm sharing it…" she quickly corrected herself. "*I was* sharing it with Vicki. She was my roommate."

"Vicki?" I asked.

"The woman just shot… *Miss Geary*," she answered with a slight quiver in her voice.

"Ya were friends then?" Red asked.

"Yes."

"For how long?"

"About two months. I'd answered an advertisement in the paper. She was looking for someone to share the rent. It's very expensive to find housing in Hollywood. Especially if you're looking for a fairly decent place."

"What kind of a person was she?" I asked.

"She was nice… kind of sweet. Very considerate of others… We got along fine."

"Did she have any friends?"

"Sure, a lot of them; mostly professional, but a few personal."

"What about boyfriends?"

"She had some men friends."

"But did she see anyone in particular?" I pressed.

"I guess, but I really can't say; she was somewhat private when it came to her personal affairs."

It may have been my imagination, but her answer seemed purposely vague.

"What about enemies?" I continued.

"Yes," Red chimed in. "Can ya think of any reason why someone would want to murder yar roommate?"

"I …," she faltered for a second, and then looking down at the ground, replied in a tiny voice, "I really can't say."

I could tell that she was suddenly feeling very uncomfortable. Either she was lying, or knew more than she was willing to tell us. I couldn't decide which.

"And what is yar position with the picture?" Red asked, and then repeated the question in a slightly different way. "What exactly is yar job here at the studio?"

"I'm an 'extra'," she replied. "I take part in the background of a scene. You know like being an individual in a crowd, or sitting in a cafe."

"How long 'ave ya been on this picture?"

"Are you asking me what time I began today?" she asked seeking clarification.

"No, I was asking how long ya been totally working on this picture?"

"This is my first day."

"Did you get the job through an agency?" I asked.

"No. I got it through Central Casting."

"And what about…" Red checked his notes. "…Miss Geary? Was this also her first day?"

"No… She has been on the set for most of the week… I believe she started last Monday… or was it Tuesday?"

"Was she also an 'extra'?"

"No. A 'bit actress'. She acted in minor roles."

"And did she get the part through an agency?"

"I don't believe so. I think somebody on the crew helped her get the job."

"Do ya know who?" Red chimed in.

"I don't." And just for a brief second she diverted her eyes.

"Are you sure?" I pressed.

She made a show of pushing a stray lock of black hair off her forehead; an attempt to buy more time before answering. She was struggling with something, but what I couldn't guess.

"Yes," she finally answered, almost in a whisper as she gazed down at some invisible point on her small, dainty feet. "Yes, I'm sure."

I wasn't buying it. Not for a thin dime! For one thing the girl was shaking like she had St. Vitus' dance and her eyes seemed to have trouble looking into mine. In the meantime I'd let her off the hook, but I made a mental note that I may need to come down harder with her at a later time.

I glanced back over to my client, who I noticed had been standing off to the side watching us. The hairdresser, Fran Adams, was still with her and they had been recently joined by the First Assistant, Don Taylor.

Adams I would describe as bookish; auburn hair done up in a bun, narrow face, straight aquiline nose and small mouth. She was wearing a plain, shapeless dress overlaid by an immaculate white smock. All she was missing, I thought with amusement, were the steel-rimmed cheaters. Taylor in contrast however, was leading man material; lean, muscular, and handsome, with straight, pearly white teeth and a Southern California tan. I had done a job for him awhile back, but quite honestly I didn't like him.

When Betty Jean had withdrawn, Miss Hyland quickly took her place.

"What's with questioning her?" she asked with a slight edge to her voice. "This is all a case of mistaken identity. You know damn well, Logan, that the victim *was supposed to be me!*"

"It sounds like you're jealous or something... Rather it had been?"

"You *know what I mean!*"

"Look... we have to investigate all angles. It's called procedure. And if you're really concerned about staying alive, you'll stay out of my way and let me do my job!"

"OK," she countered, a slight flush spreading across her face, "but don't forget who's paying you!" And with that she stormed away.

'Daddy's girl', I summed up. She undoubtedly was used to getting her own way. I'd continue on with this investigation, but fifty dollars or not, I was not playing babysitter to a spoiled child. If she planned to play that game, she'd have to get her own pabulum!

While my client and I had been talking, Red had gathered some of the crew and was methodically questioning them. As I joined their circle, he stated, "The prop man reported seeing a guy leave da studio moments after the murder…" He went on to give a description. "Did anyone else see him… or perhaps know who he is?"

Fran Adams spoke up.

"He has been hanging around the studio the last few days… never said a word to anyone as far as I know. He just hung out in the background and watched what went on, on the set."

"And no idea who he is, or why he was here?" Red looked from one to the other.

"I heard talk," Soames piped up, "that he might have some connections with the producer. Maybe to keep an eye on the money or something."

"I heard more," Taylor added. It was the first time that he'd spoken, and there was something in his tone that particularly caught my attention.

"And what was that?" I asked.

"That he had mob connections."

It was possible. It wouldn't be the first time that "dirty" money was invested in a picture.

"I don't think he's with the mob," Soames inter-jected quickly. He'd said it with such conviction that I had to ask why not? His response was less sure, "I don't know, just doesn't look the gangster type."

I wasn't sure about that, but I let it pass.

"Did anyone see him hanging around da prop boxes anytime during da morning shooting?" Red in-quired, again gazing questioningly about their faces.

There was a pause, as collectively they all searched their memories.

"Yes… I believe I did see him there!" It was Taylor again.

"Around the time of the murder?" I asked quickly.

"It could have been, but I can't be sure."

"But, he was over there?"

"Yes. I can say so definitely."

Red had a couple of officers collect the names, ad-dresses, and statements from the group, as the boys from the crime lab finished up their work and the body was removed to the coroner's meat wagon.

He specifically ordered the witnesses not to leave town, unless of course by his permission, and to avoid any discussion amongst themselves regarding the crime until the course of the investigation was completed. When they all nodded their assent, he dismissed them.

I caught the eye of Soames and waved him over.

"What did you find out?"

"One of the weapons had been fired, a .38 caliber Smith and Wesson revolver. I gave it to the inspector."

"Did anyone witness you giving him the weapon?"

"No. I brought him over to the property area. I'm pretty sure we were alone."

"And you didn't happen to mention finding it to anybody?"

He shook his head.

"Good. For the sake of the investigation we would like to keep that information confidential." I then instructed him, "Don't tell anyone what you found, no matter how innocent they may seem." Again, I warned, "keep this strictly between us."

He solemnly agreed.

"Then it's just a matter for ballistics to match the bullet with the weapon," I finished more to myself than him. "Thanks."

At which point, he walked away.

I searched out Red, who seemed to be concluding the day's investigations.

"You're planning to wrap it up?" I asked as I walked up to him.

"Yes, Thomas," he replied. "I think we've done all dat could be done around here. A deep business this is. I think this one is going to take some digging."

I agreed, and he told me to keep in touch.

"Mister Logan?" I was so deep in thought as I watched Red walk away that I didn't notice Betty Jean at my elbow. I looked down and was surprised to see real terror in her eyes. "We need to talk. Something's not right here... and quite honestly... I fear for my life."

4

THE LURKING DANGER

I've walked the streets of Hollywood with all its tinsel and glitter...and looked into the innocent faces of kids who came from every corner of the world with dreams of instant fame. For most, it was like reaching for a dandelion... one puff and it's gone.

And what about the others? The individuals fortunate enough to actually reach that pinnacle of success? If they're smart they'll keep their nose clean and life will be as smooth as glass, but unfortunately few ever do. Most become partakers of the seven deadly sins, seduced by the party world of drugs, booze, and loose dames; destructive urges, which can spontaneously ignite and create a fire so consuming that it will eventually burn out their soul and leave them as a charred, hollow

*frame. In the process laws will be broken,
and the seduced will be driven to extremes,
committing the most heinous of crimes…even
murder as a device to suit their wicked ways.*

That was the second time in two days that I
heard that line. Only this time after what had
just occurred I was taking this call for help
more seriously. The girl was shaking from head to toe,
and I couldn't help but try to comfort her.

"Could you be more specific?" I asked gently. "If
you give me a few details I might be able to help you."

"I could. But, not here." She tore a piece of paper
from a notepad she had in her purse and wrote an address on it. "Do you have a car?" she asked, handing
me the paper after first folding it neatly in half.

"Yeah, several," I answered shortly. "The Hollywood
Boulevard Line, the Venice Short Line…. in short, the
Los Angeles Pacific Electric street car system. Why?"

"Because after we talk there is something I have
to show you. And we'll need to go to Santa Monica to
collect it."

I thought for a moment, and then responded, "I
probably could borrow one. A friend of mine has an
automobile I swear he only drives on Sundays. What
time were you thinking?"

"I heard they plan to 'wrap' around six…" She
thought for a second and then suggested, "Seven thirty?"

"Sure." I placed my hands gently on her shoulders. "In the meantime, are you going to be OK?"

She nodded slowly at first, and then with some conviction.

"We have a movie to make!" the director shouted over his megaphone in an attempt to regain control over the production. "I need everyone back on the set!"

She started to move away when I caught her by the elbow. I had a final question, and it couldn't wait. I'd noticed that 'Script' was written across the back of the chair where the victim had been sitting. That got me thinking.

"I know these movie types are particular about who sits where. How did Miss Geary end up in the chair assigned to Hyland?"

"Vicki... Miss Geary, was feeling light headed. I went over to her when I saw she wasn't feeling well, and then brought it to…"

She stopped suddenly. Something over my shoulder had caught her attention.

"Excuse me," Don Taylor interrupted, "but the director wants you on the set."

"Thank you," she answered sharply. "I'll be right there."

As he walked away, I directed her attention back to our conversation.

"You were saying?"

"The director…Mr. Clemmons; I brought Vicki's condition to his attention," she replied, with a marked nervous rise in her voice. "I believe it was he that told her to sit in Miss Hyland's chair and then ordered Miss Hyland to fetch some water. They had a bottle of it over at Craft Services on the far end of the lot."

I remembered my client, Hyland, holding a glass when I looked up from the body, so at least that part of her story checked.

I arrived in her neighborhood just slightly before seven thirty. I parked the large, maroon Packard in front of the Hollywood Hotel located at the corner of Hollywood and Highland, and hiked the three blocks east to her apartment complex.

The building and grounds were both designed in the old Spanish Hacienda style, complete with white-washed adobe siding, red tiled roof and tall over-hanging palms. A high stucco wall surrounded the complex, which included a small garden located toward the front and accessed through an archway spanned by a black, wrought iron gate. I noted the words 'Casa de Flores' painted on a piece of tile secured to the left of the entrance.

Metal hinges squealed in protest as I pushed open the gate and then shut with a loud clang as it swung closed solidly behind. I stepped out onto a narrow cement pathway, bordered on either side by beds of colorful flowers, ferns and tall grass. The two-storied apartment building stood just ahead, encompassing three sides of a square adobe brick patio. All the apartment doors faced out toward this central patio and could be reached by climbing a flight of red tiled stairs. These were located on either side of the building, and both led up to a narrow balcony that wrapped around the entire second floor. Her apartment was on this upper level, number 201.

It was a warm evening, and sounds from the surrounding apartments carried down to where I was standing. I particularly could make out music coming from a radio, 'Rudy Vallee and the Yankees', a new variety show presented by Standard Brands, and it seemed to be drifting from her apartment. It became louder as I climbed the stairs and neared her door... so noisy that I figured on knocking hard so I could be heard over the racket. To my surprise the solid wooden door swung slightly open at my first rap. Apparently it was already ajar.

Immediately I sensed the hairs rise on my neck. From where I stood the room was dark. Carefully I reached over and swung the door slightly wider. In a pool of moonlight that filtered through one of the windows, I spotted Betty Jean sitting bolt upright in a chair squarely facing me in the doorway. Fear was etched on her face and her chest rose and sunk in short shallow breaths. I could tell that she wanted to say something but couldn't find her voice, paralyzed as she was in terror. I took a step further into the room, and that was when it happened. The world before my eyes exploded into a bright piercing light that was soon followed by a deep absorbing pool of inky black darkness.

I found myself swimming in this void, my arms and legs attempting to tread water, but neither responding. It took every ounce of energy just to keep afloat. In the distance, a small point of gray light appeared and instinctively I knew it would bring safety if only I could reach it. My efforts toward it however had proven fruitless, yet in time, I noticed it starting to come closer of its own accord. And bringing with it something besides … something I didn't expect; pain, like a thousand jackhammers pounding inside my skull. Perhaps, I reasoned, I was better off in the darkness. But then, I wasn't in control, and incapable of turning back now even if I wanted to. As the light encompassed me, my memory returned, and instantly my senses started to take account of my predicament.

I was face down, flat on a tile floor, and when I felt strong enough to open my eyes, verified that I was lying spread eagle a few feet inside the apartment just in front of the doorway. I lifted my head slightly, the action causing a spasm of pain shooting down the length of my spine. My vision was blurred, but I could just make out a shadowy form rummaging through the apartment: a large frame outlined by the dim illumination of the flashlight he carried. I could also see by this same beam the body of Betty Jean, the abnormal angle of her head leaving a sick, empty feeling in the pit of my stomach. This was the second one I was too late for, which stirred my anger.

Seeing red, I was making ready to rush the figure, when rising up on unsteady knees I caught the sensation of a faint breeze behind me. Suddenly the front door swung fully open and I was knocked violently back onto the floor by a rushing figure who stormed through its opening. A short confrontation followed, whereas this new intruder was knocked aside as the killer, who, taking advantage of the occasion, bolted out the door and into the night.

I started to feel dizzy, the recent kick to my ribs not helping the situation, and was on the point of passing out when I caught one detail… a red scarf trailing from the intruder's neck as he gave chase to the fleeing killer.

"He's OK," I heard a familiar voice say. "Dat head wouldn't yield to anything less than a mallet!"

I opened one eye slightly and caught sight of Red's ugly mug split into a wide grin.

"I should have guessed," I mumbled sarcastically. "Saint Peter would have shown more compassion!"

"And last I checked," he added, "I don't think he was Irish…. Well, maybe on his mother's side."

I raised myself to a sitting position and fought off the wave of nausea that accompanied the mild dizziness I was feeling.

"Boy, I could sure use an aspirin!" I exclaimed as I felt the goose egg on the back of my head. Red signaled over to the doctor who was attending Betty Jean's body. He went off for some water.

"Da place is a mess," Red commented as we waited for the doctor to return. "It also looks like da girl was worked over pretty good, too. Seemed he was looking for something. Any ideas?"

"Nope." I answered, holding my head. "But I'm pretty sure he didn't find it."

"How's that?" he asked.

Just then the doctor returned with the pills and water. Red had to wait until I took them before I answered. "Because Betty Jean indicated that there was something she wanted to show me in Santa Monica…. And that I suspect is what the killer's after." A thought suddenly occurred to me. "By the way, how did you end up here?"

"Someone called da station. They didn't identify themselves. They just reported da crime."

"Male or female?" I asked quickly.

"Male," he replied. "You know something?"

I went on to describe the incident that had just occurred.

"Him again," he replied in answer to my observation of the scarf. "Saint or sinner, dat's the question."

"Exactly."

I glanced over at the coroner examining her body. This case was starting to gnaw at my guts. If a bullet wasn't bad enough, now this animal was beating up on little girls. What a cold, ruthless bastard he must be. This no longer was just a job to me. It had just turned into something more personal. However long it took, and whatever the consequences, I was going to make sure that he'd pay. Even if it took my dying breath to do so.

"Did she give you any idea where in Santa Monica she wanted to take you?"

Red caught me off guard. I was so lost in my anger that it took me a second to understand what he was asking, and even then I asked him to repeat the question. When he did, I stuttered in response, "Unfortunately, no."

"Too bad," he replied. "It would have made our job easier."

Again I felt the fire build up inside of me. "I just can't get over how stupid I was. All the warning signs were there... I even saw some of them, *and still* I walked into the trap!" I cussed. "He was behind the door...oldest trick in the book...and if I would have thought before I acted, that poor girl might still be alive to tell us."

Just then one of the attending officers came over with a small bag in his hand.

"I think you might want to see this, sir," he said handing over the object to Red. "The coroner found it in the victim's mouth."

He opened the bag. "What da...?" He looked puzzled. "It's a matchbook!"

And so it was. Now this case was really becoming bizarre.

5

THE UNUSUAL CLUE

It's funny how the mind works. Here's a girl faced with the inevitability of death and she focuses her last conscious moments trying to preserve a secret on the one hand, and yet find a way to pass it on in another. Why? Was it her way of getting back at her tormentor, or was it due to a sense of duty. Or maybe in a roundabout way she felt that it might somehow label her killer. I'd like to think that it might be all of the above.

A match folder! I looked over to the desk where her chair had been standing. A collection of matchbooks stored in a glass bowl was overturned and a dozen or more were spread across the blotter. Sometime during her ordeal when she was not being watched, or perhaps in her last dying moments as the killer was searching elsewhere, she used the diversion to select this particular set of matches to conceal in her mouth. You had to hand it to this brave girl; even in pain and facing death she still had the ability to think clearly. I had no doubt that she was trying to send a message. There was no other explanation, unless it served some purpose of the killer, which didn't make any sense. No, I reasoned. A message from her was the only conclusion.

Red tilted the bag and let the folder fall out onto the desk. With a handkerchief he carefully turned it so we could see the image printed on the cover. It was an etching of a merry-go-round and the words **Carousel Diner** was printed across its length.

"I know dat diner!" Red exclaimed. "It's located downtown."

"Yes," I replied, "but remember what we're looking for is in Santa Monica. I think I might have an idea." I started to search for my hat. "I have a car outside… are you game for an excursion?"

I looked at my watch. It was just ten o'clock.

"I don't think you should go anywhere until someone takes a look at dat skull."

I pointed to my head and asked him, "You see it?"

"Yes," he replied suspiciously.

"Then good… it's been looked at!" I started for the door. He grabbed my arm.

"Look," he said seriously, "dats a nasty bump. You could 'ave a concussion!"

"We don't have time!" I exclaimed, growing impatient. "It can wait." He still wouldn't budge, so I went on to explain, "We don't know if the girl had talked. I sort of doubt it, because the murderer was still searching after he'd killed her. Nevertheless, we can't take that chance. He could have the jump on us, which means we better get moving!"

"I believe yar might be right, me boy," he finally relented, "but I drive. You're a hazard on da road normally, but with dat bump on yar head… well, ya might get dizzy and I don't want to end up spending da rest of me evening in a ditch!"

Red followed my directions to Santa Monica and parked the car a block away from the pier. It was a Friday night and the amusement area was packed with visitors. As we walked down the slope that led to the beginning of the boardwalk, I indicated 'The Hippodrome', a Byzantine-Moorish style structure off to our left. This building housed the popular carousel. Pointing it out I said, "I think we'll find our answer there."

The Santa Monica Municipal Pier was opened in 1909 after sixteen months of construction. Within a few years an amusement boardwalk was built adjacent to it just to the south. A number of thrill rides were added, including a large coaster called the Whirlwind Dipper, one of the fastest on the Pacific Coast. Arcades were also constructed, as well as the La Monica Ballroom, which featured the latest bands providing the best in dance music. The newest attraction these days, however, was "Muscle Beach," a place for bodybuilders to go and work on their biceps.

By the time we reached the entrance to 'The Hippodrome' we were already surrounded by a mixture of colorful lights, loud talk, laughter, music, and the occasional scream— each carried by the warm, summer night breeze. We pushed open the door that led to the piers' beautiful merry-go-round, highly detailed down to its hand-carved painted ponies and chariots. Calliope music brightened the scene accented by the giggles of the young riders. I searched out the operator and upon finding him, asked where I could find the manager. He directed us to an office located in the back.

"Excuse me." I flashed my card and Clancy his buzzer. "But, could we bother you for a moment?"

An older gentleman looked up over his glasses from where he sat poring through some ledgers at a large oak desk.

"Sure," he responded uncertain. "What can I do for you?"

"We're here on police business," Red announced. "Two women 'ave been murdered in da last twelve hours, and a piece of evidence has led us here."

"You must explain," he mumbled with a slight nervous quiver. "I know nothing about a murder. I've been here all day."

"Do ya know a woman named Geary?" Red asked.

"Yes, I have heard the name," he responded cautiously. "She's my niece's roommate."

"Then Betty Jean is your niece?"

"Yes." He then added with concern, "she's not involved in this, is she?"

"I'm afraid she's dead."

At the mention of Betty Jean's death the elder paled, and for a moment I thought he was going to pass out. Red waited until the man had regained his composure before continuing.

"I'm sorry we had to break it to you dis way," Red began gently, "but she left a message before she died and it has led us here."

The old man seemed understandably confused, and I was afraid close to shock. I decided to chime in and get him talking about something he felt comfortable about. It usually helped.

"Could you tell us something about your niece?"

He looked up at me blankly. I could tell that he was fighting tears, but after a moment he began weakly, "Betty Jean wasn't her full name. It was Williams... Betty Jean Williams. She's my sister's daughter." He stopped and swallowed hard. "She moved here about two months ago from Little Falls, Minnesota. The family wasn't crazy about it, but she got this fool idea into her head that she was going to make it in pictures. Become a star like her idol Harlow. We knew it was silly, but there was no convincing her otherwise."

This was the typical dream of most young girls living in small town America, which nine times out of ten usually resulted in bitter disappointment. Fortunately, not too many of these situations had ended up like Betty Jean's. The usual scenario being rejection, loss, and near destitution, forcing them to seek some menial job, usually at some two-bit café where after spending endless nights waiting on tables and dealing with some sleazy characters, they finally reach their decision. Disillusioned by their unfulfilled dreams of stardom they seek out the nearest bus station where they bought themselves a ticket back home, 'one way.'

"The family wanted her to stay with me," he continued, "but that was impossible. My apartment was too small, and it didn't seem proper. She found this ad in the paper advertising for a roommate... that's how she found this apartment with Miss Geary." He paused again, shaking his head. We waited patiently as he struggled to get hold of his emotions, but it was becoming all too obvious that it was increasingly more difficult for him.

He started ranting, "I can't help feeling responsible. Maybe I should've watched her more closely."

I wanted to be as delicate as possible. I could understand his dilemma. Being her only relative in Los Angeles, he no doubt felt responsible. But these self-remonstrations were not getting us anywhere; we needed to proceed with the investigation and the pertinent questions had to be asked. Time was of the essence, so I cut to the chase.

"Have you seen your niece lately?"

The question drew him back to reality and seemed to calm him.

"Yes, just the other night."

"And did she have something with her? Perhaps a package or a letter she wanted you to keep?"

"She did as a matter of fact." He seemed surprised.

I looked over at Red who gave me a knowing grin, and then turned back toward the uncle and said, "Tell us about it."

He indicated a couple of chairs and we sat. In a somber tone he began relating to us the details of her last visit. He said that she had come to his office Wednesday night around closing. She had not called ahead and seemed relieved when she found he was still there. He felt that she seemed nervous and most anxious to be rid of a package that was left in her keeping.

I interrupted him at this point. "Did she say who the package belonged to?"

"Yes. It was her roommate's... Miss Geary's."

"Did she say why it was left in her keeping?" Red interjected.

"Just that her roommate was afraid someone would steal it. She said that Miss Geary felt it was not safe in their apartment... that she suspected an attempt was made to steal it that same afternoon."

"Did she say how?"

"Only that there was an unsuccessful attempt to force the lock on the front door."

"And do you still have this package?" I asked.

"Yes," he replied.

"May we see it?"

Reluctant at first, he eventually retrieved the parcel from a niche located behind one of his bookcases. It was a medium sized package wrapped in plain brown paper and sealed with string. I noticed that one of the edges was torn across its length and some of the string loosened.

"Did you open it?" I asked.

"No. It was that way when she handed it to me."

If that was true, then it only followed that Betty Jean's curiosity must've gotten the better of her. Tempted, she had taken a look for herself… a case of Pandora opening the box, which unfortunately had ended with the same consequences.

We told him that it would be necessary for us to unwrap it, which we did in his presence. Inside was a leather-bound book… a journal to be exact. It had a catch, but it wasn't locked. Red looked over my shoulder as I thumbed through it.

"Bunch of mumbo jumbo," he finally commented after viewing several of the pages, which seemed to be filled with a mixture of scribbles, crudely drawn pictures, and numbers…lots of numbers. "What do ya make of it?"

"I don't know?" I responded. "Could be a type of shorthand, and the pictures might be pictograms." He looked quizzically at me. "A type of children's puzzle."

Just then a bank slip dropped from one of its pages.

Red picked it up and held it to the desk lamp. "Deposit receipt for a thousand dollars, cash. It's dated for this last Monday."

"'Bout the only thing that makes sense about this whole package," I concluded finally. "The signature is Geary's. You can probably get an injunction." I pointed to the account number printed on the slip. "This will be of help."

I thanked the old gentleman for his cooperation and explained that the book would have to be taken as evidence. We told him that he should check with the coroner tomorrow in regards to the release of his niece's body, and warned that there might be some delay depending upon the progress of the investigation.

When we reached the car, I commented, "This is a part of the business I don't think I'll ever get used to. I can handle some petty crook getting shived in an alleyway, but I can never stomach some innocent person being stiffed for being in the wrong place at the wrong time. And I like it less when we have to break it to their relatives."

"Don't go soft on me, Thomas," Red warned. "Are you really sure dat she is innocent?" I reluctantly shook my head. "Then you see, you're breaking da first cardinal rule of objective investigation; never draw conclusions before da facts, and never let emotions cloud your judgment." He patted me on the back. "Now, what about dis book?"

I sat for a moment, thinking and then responded, "Is Mary Kelly still with the department?"

"Sure, she's in da steno pool. Why?"

"Because, as I recall she was a wiz when it came to solving puzzles. Crosswords, Cryptograms, you name it. She was quite good at it. Let her take a shot of making some sense of those scribbles."

"Dat sounds like a plan," he conceded. "And in da meantime I will follow up with Miss Geary's bank account." He started the car. "What's your next move? Get dat head of yours checked out?"

"My head *is fine*! All I need is a good night's sleep, and then tomorrow I think I will try to go back to the studio and get a lead on a missing script."

"I didn't know one had disappeared," he commented as he pulled into traffic.

"It had to. Somebody cut up one to compose that letter threatening my client, and it's an even bet that if we find that script it may lead to our killer!"

6

STALKED BY DEATH

Up to this point I had been, quite honestly, "winging it"… following along to wherever the circumstances had led me. But now I had formulated a plan; a systematic method that I would take to get at the truth of this crime. Now my investigation would begin in earnest!

My apartment was situated in the *Somerset Arms* atop Bunker Hill. I'd originally selected the building because it was located near my former job with the Los Angeles Police Department. Now that my office was situated on Hollywood Boulevard, the location wasn't as convenient. Still the place had charm, and the rent was affordable. It was close to the Angels Flight, a funicular proclaimed one of the shortest railways in the world. For two bits you can ride on either of two, orange and black railcars, the "Olivet" and "Sinai," that climb a 350-foot slope up the side of the hill. The entrance to my building was located close to the upper station.

I had slept pretty well that night despite my injuries, and woke up relieved that I no longer had a headache. The bump had gone down with the help of an ice pack, and was only partially sore from a cut caused by the 'sap' I was hit with. I retrieved the L.A. *Times* from outside my apartment door, a perk courtesy of the management. The previous day's murders were a front page item. I looked briefly over the article, noting that the police were searching for our "mystery man" who was now categorized by them as a "person of interest." Tossing the paper aside, I went about preparing my usual breakfast. It consisted of Kellogg's "Pep" cereal, sliced oranges, toast, and piping hot cups of Chase and Sanborn coffee. As I removed the bottle of milk from my ice box, I happened to glance at the label: "Hyland Milk." It reminded me that I hadn't heard my client's account of yesterday's tragedy and placed that on my mental "to do" list for the next couple of days. However, for the immediate future I wanted to follow up on that script angle, and after finishing my meal, promptly dialed the exchange who rang up the studio. I was told by a secretary that the company was not shooting today, but that all the crew was still on site for a production meeting. I made an appointment for 11 o'clock.

After showering, shaving, and quickly dressing, I caught a street car that would take me to the studio. I had left the automobile I had borrowed last night parked in front of my apartment. By arrangement, my old buddy was to pick it up at noon.

It was a slow journey, but having left early I was still able to reach the studio's front gate by 10:45. I checked in and asked for directions to the production office. I noted that he was the same guard from my last visit, and figuring that he was on duty during the day of the murder, asked if he remembered a man with a red scarf passing through the front gate.

"About my height, perhaps slightly smaller," I explained, "heavy coat and tan fedora. Overdresses for the warm weather, and doesn't seem to vary his apparel. Some of the people I've interviewed indicated that he'd been hanging around the studio for some days. If you saw him I'm sure you would remember him."

"I'm sure I would, too," he replied shaking his head. "But quite honestly I can't recall anyone of that description ever coming through the gate."

"Is there anyone else on duty here during the day?"

"No, I'm the only one. I've been on the day shift for the last six months," he explained, pointing to a schedule attached to a peg on the wall. "I get a relief for half an hour at lunch; otherwise I'm at this post from six a.m. to three-thirty p.m."

"What time do you take lunch?"

"About one."

"So, you would have been at the gate during the time of the murder?"

"Yes sir. Sometime after ten, correct?"

I nodded.

"And you're sure that you saw no one of that description leave?" I repeated. "I'd imagine he'd be in a hurry, so you couldn't miss him."

"I'm positive," he responded with confidence. "I can check over the 'sign in' lists," he volunteered, "and talk to Ed and Terry; they work the other shifts. See if they know anything."

I told him that would be helpful, and then asked, "Aside from passing through these gates, would there be any other way for someone to get into the studio?"

"Sure. It's possible. We're not exactly a federal bank. If they knew a person on the inside they might be able to manage it." He then added as an afterthought, "Though I couldn't exactly be able to tell you how."

I thanked him, and he took my card with the promise that he would contact me if he discovered anything further.

This case wasn't going to provide any easy answers. I'd have to resign myself to that fact. It always seemed that the jobs which began so straightforwardly, usually ended up the most difficult to unravel. I couldn't help but keep these happy thoughts in mind as I made my way toward the Production Office.

"Is there something I can do for you?" the long-legged brunette asked as I walked into the reception room. There was something in the way she uttered it that seemed to say more than the words she was mouthing. She was that species of dame who found everything that walked in pants a challenge. I guess the best and the simplest description that I could give of her was "a flirt." Normally, I wouldn't mind playing at her game. She was attractive, but I just couldn't get two other equally nice looking girls who were now lying stiff in a morgue out of my mind. That's why I decided to stick strictly to the job. No monkey business today for this detective.

"Who handles the scripts around here…specifically for the "Keys to Adventure" picture, and how do they get distributed?"

"I do," she replied, after flashing a disarming smile.

I pulled up a chair so it faced her desk.

"Great," I said after getting seated. "Do you personally hand them out? And is there some type of system for their distribution?"

She answered "yes" to both accounts. They were particularly concerned with "outsiders" getting hold of the story, especially with a production of this caliber, and took extra precautions to ensure protecting its rights. Therefore, each script was given a number and then specifically assigned to each crew member. A limited number was released, and only to those who absolutely needed one.

"And did any go missing?"

She blinked her long dark eyelashes. "Why, yes. I did have to replace one."

"Whose?" I asked quickly.

"Mr. Clemmons."

The Director; now that I found interesting. I asked if he was around and she said that he was in the next office meeting with his staff.

"Could I talk with him for a few minutes after he's finished?"

She told me that she would check, and then rising from her chair made an elaborate show of smoothing a crease in her dress, her eyes locking teasingly onto mine. She took a couple steps into the room and then turned to see if I was watching. I was. And again I had to remind myself that I was here for business, deadly serious business! She disappeared into the other room for several minutes, and then returned with a message that he would be available in about an hour.

As she settled herself back behind her desk I asked, "Were you acquainted with either of the murdered women?"

"Miss Geary had stopped by to collect the pages of her script. I never saw the other girl."

"Pages?" I asked.

"Yes," she replied. "We don't pass out a full script for actors who have only a few lines; just those pages that have their dialogue on it." She thought a second. "Her's was only a couple of pages."

"Could you think of any reasons why someone would want to kill either of these women?" It was a long shot, but people love to gossip and it could be useful what she might've learned hanging around the water cooler. She shook her head however.

"Did Miss Geary come to the office other than to collect her dialogue?"

"I don't believe so."

"Not even for her interview?" I offered. "Actors usually audition, don't they?"

"She didn't. They usually go through me... but I think she was flat out hired."

"By whom?" I asked.

"I don't know," she answered simply.

"Does she have an agent?"

"Yes." She started fumbling through a small file box on her table. After thumbing through it a couple of times she finally found what she was looking for, an index card with information regarding Geary's agent. I copied the information into my notebook.

Having concluded my interview with time to spare, I asked my flirtatious beauty, whose name I learned was Rita, whether I could wander around the studio while I waited for Clemmons to finish his meeting.

"Sure, I don't think that would be a problem as long as you stay out of the areas posted 'prohibited.' And watch out for any red warning lights near the entrances to the sound stages. Don't go in while they're lit; it means they're shooting."

"I'll remember that," I replied smiling. "Any other advice?"

"You might want to visit the commissary and get some coffee," she suggested, and then added coyly, "I'd take you there myself if I wasn't so busy."

I had to hand it to this kid, she was certainly persistent!

I started for the door, but stopped as an idea suddenly occurred to me. Turning back, I asked, "Do you know if Dick Soames is around?"

"Yes, I believe so. He's been in and out of here several times this morning."

"Where can I find him?"

She considered the question briefly, and then answered,

"Probably in the warehouse."

I asked for directions, which she drew roughly as a map on a sheet of paper and then handed it to me folded. As I stepped outside I opened it, noting with amusement that she had included her name and phone number in prominent script along the bottom.

It was a Saturday, so the lot was pretty deserted. As a rule, filming took place on the weekdays leaving the sixth for preparation work by the production team and staff. Sunday everyone had off. I followed her directions to the letter and located the large, stucco building that housed the 'Property Department' as it announced in painted letters on one corner of the facade. I walked up the ramp that led to its entrance which faced out onto a large loading dock. No one seemed to be in the front office, so I wandered inside. It was dark, musty, and claustrophobic. Objects of every kind could be found stacked floor to ceiling along numerous aisles that ran the length of the building. Various pieces of furniture were even hung from the ceiling, and paintings, with or without frames, lined the walls.

"Hello!" I called out into the darkness. Only my hail echoed back.

I slowly advanced farther down the aisle, my surroundings getting murkier with every step. At one point I felt that I was being watched, but then noticed the several mounted moose heads facing in my direction. I continued on, the sensation of the solid Colt .45 holstered securely under my arm bolstering my confidence.

"Hello!" I shouted again, and this time I thought I caught the sound of a door shutting quietly behind me. I turned and called out, but was still only greeted by silence. I advanced. It wasn't until I had reached about midway into the building that I heard a sharp grinding sound that was quite close and somewhere above me. At that instant, I spied a large plaster urn tilting dangerously forward from the upper storage shelf. I reacted, but not quick enough to prevent it from pinning me under as it came crashing to the floor.

"Are you all right?" Soames asked alarmed. He seemed to appear out of nowhere. Immediately he started to lift the object off me. "What happened?"

"I don't know. I was searching for you, calling out, and then this vase came crashing down on me." I watched his expression carefully as I related the incident.

"Strange thing to happen," he replied while looking convincingly perplexed. "It should've been pretty secure up there. It shouldn't have tipped on its own like that. It's not like we had an earthquake or something."

I was going to answer that 'I thought that it was more likely pushed,' but thought better of it. If the urn had been made of cement the situation might have turned out much differently, but as it stood now, it had just momentarily knocked the wind out of me.

"Sorry I didn't answer you," he continued. "I was in the office on the other side of the building. I had the radio on, and I guess I didn't hear you. I was on the phone, too. Strange thing, I answered it and was told to wait, but no one came on again."

"Any idea who it was?" I asked quickly.

"It was a male voice, but I couldn't recognize it." He then added, "Why? Does it mean anything?"

"Probably not," I replied, purposely being vague.

I told him that I had some questions that I wanted to ask him and he escorted me back to his office.

"Brandy?" he offered.

Why not? I wouldn't pretend that the incident hadn't un-nerved me, which incidentally, I reasoned, was all it was probably designed to do. I accepted the glass.

"I'm glad you stopped by," Soames began, as he poured one for himself. "I've discovered something unusual since I'd talked to you last."

"What was that?" I asked.

"Well, I found one of my revolvers, a British Webley, tossed in one of the barrels on the set."

"Any idea how it got there?"

"I don't have a clue," he replied, taking a sip of his drink. "Although I'm sure it was the weapon I'd collected from an 'extra' who was released earlier that day."

"Was that before or after the murder?"

"Before," he answered shortly. However, I remember leaving it on the edge of the bench. How it ended up in a barrel is a real mystery."

"Was there any rounds in it?"

"Just blanks. I checked."

"Were any fired?"

"I examined that as well. I knew the 'extra' hadn't fired it, and I was curious if it had been misused in some way. There were no marks on any of the primers, so I'm sure it wasn't fired."

Interesting, but I couldn't see how it related to the murder. I decided to move on.

"As I recall you said you were standing over by the sound booth when the shot was fired. Why there? Why not over in the property area? Weren't you nervous about leaving all those weapons unguarded?"

"In answer to your first question, the director specifically asked me to watch how the 'extras' were handling their weapons. I couldn't supervise properly from the prop area. It was too far away. I needed a full view of the action, and the spot near the booth was the perfect location." He took another sip of his drink. "Now regarding that second question; if we'd been out on location I might've been concerned, but we were on a closed studio lot and seeing that we hadn't had any history of thefts, I wasn't all that worried about their safety."

Fair enough answer. I thought I'd ask another.

"Can you think of any reason why someone would want to kill Miss Geary?" He shook his head. "What about Miss Hyland?"

"Mattie?" he asked, markedly surprised. "Who would want to kill Mattie?"

"That's what I'm trying to find out. She received a note threatening her life just a few days ago."

"I'd no idea," he replied, and the answer seemed genuine.

"It's possible that Geary was mistaken for Hyland yesterday and that's why she was killed."

"I heard another girl was murdered. She was an 'extra' on our set. I believe her name was Betty Jean. Was there a connection?"

"Might be. How'd you hear of it?"

"Word gets around."

Pretty vague, but I decided not to pursue it further. Instead I asked, "Were you aware that Miss Geary was feeling ill, or did you notice anything happening where she was standing either prior to, or after the shot was fired?"

He shook his head, but I could tell that the question made him feel uneasy.

"As I mentioned before, the only thing out of the ordinary I noticed was that man running away from the scene."

"And you don't recall anything about Miss Geary?" I pressed. "For instance had you seen her on the set earlier?"

He paused as if weighing his next answer.

"We obviously crossed paths once or twice earlier, in-between shootings."

"And when was that exactly?"

He paused again. "I believe it was first thing that morning and again just before the last 'set up', the scene they were shooting when she was killed."

"Tell me about it." I wanted him to be more specific.

"Not much to tell." He was being evasive.

I wasn't letting him off the hook.

"Where did you see her?"

"Around," he stated curtly, and when he sensed I wasn't happy with his answer, then reluctantly added, "perhaps, Craft Service."

"Both times?"

"Yes."

"What was she doing there?"

"She was getting coffee like the rest of us." I sensed some agitation in his answer.

"Both times?" I asked, seeking further clarification. "Did she get one that afternoon?"

"I'm not certain, she might have. No, on second thought, I don't think so."

I found it interesting. He seemed to be having trouble with a simple question.

"Are you sure?" I asked, leaning on him harder. "You seem confused."

"No. I'm pretty sure. She only got coffee that morning."

He was trying to sound confident, but it wasn't convincing. His evasiveness was giving him away. Obviously he was trying to hide something. The questions were what and why?

7

A SCRIPTED THREAT

Most times when you feed a tiger he becomes lazy and docile. That's why I am always particularly suspicious when a potential suspect wines and dines me. Are they really concerned about what they put into my mouth, or what may come out of theirs?

J ack Clemmons was waiting for me when I returned to the production office. He wasn't a tall man, about 5'6" or 5'7". He was well built; tan; about early fifties, with blond hair which was thinning. He was handsome in a rugged sort of way; thin, chiseled mouth, hawk-like nose, strong chin, and cold gray eyes. As soon as I walked in he informed me that he was starving and invited me to lunch, his treat. Needless to say, I took him up on the offer.

"I thought we might lunch at the Brown Derby," he said as we waited for a driver from 'Transportation' to pick us up. He had called from his office, and we were now standing at the curb in front of the Production Building. "Not the restaurant in Hollywood. I reserve that for business deals. I much prefer the original on Wilshire." It sounded fine to me; after all, he was picking up the tab!

A dark sedan pulled up and a driver jumped out. As he held open the rear door, a strange feeling suddenly came over me. There was something very familiar about this car. I had the distinct impression that I'd seen it before, let's say, outside my office a couple of days prior.

"Is this your car?" I asked as nonchalantly as possible, making a show of admiring it, but actually trying to get a glance at the license.

"No. Not personally; it belongs to the studio. We have a fleet of these that are available to employees." The plate was commercial. So that checked.

We drove off in silence and it wasn't until we'd gone several blocks that I attempted to reopen the conversation. "The reason I stopped by to see you is that I have some questions regarding that incident at the studio yesterday."

"Sure. Fire away."

"OK," I said, organizing my thoughts. "Where exactly were you at the time of the murder?"

"Where I should be," he responded, "next to the camera watching the action on the set."

"So you were not aware of any events leading up to the murder?"

"Like, for instance?" he asked.

"That Miss Geary was feeling ill just prior to being shot?"

"Not at all." He was firm in his response.

"Now, that's odd, because I was told that it was you who ordered that the victim be seated, and likewise had suggested that Miss Hyland be sent to get some water for her."

"Then your source is wrong, or lying." he replied with marked agitation. "Ask them again."

"I can't. I'm afraid the girl is dead."

He just stared at me. At that point we pulled up to the front of the restaurant.

The original 'Brown Derby' was established about three and a half years ago. Its distinctive façade designed to resemble the brown derby of its name. This style of architecture was meant to draw the attention of passing motorists, which it did, and also gain it the instant recognition of tourists from around the world.

We were shown to a booth by the maitre d', who left us with a large multi-paged menu. After making my selection I gazed with fascination about the establishment, soaking in the rich, elegant atmosphere, which on my budget was an exceedingly rare sight.

The room had black leathered upholstered booths surrounding tables covered with spotless white linen, and set with highly polished silverware, delicate china, and heavy carved crystal. A number of black wrought ironed chandeliers surrounded by a dozen or more candle shaped lamps provided illumination. Each individual light was covered by its own shade to create a warm, inviting glow. The walls were also notable, embossed with a paper of a subtle cream color and dignified richness, upon which hung either photographic portraits or numerous sketches of movie actors and actresses from the silent era to the present day, many of these personally autographed by the subjects.

After we placed our orders with the immaculately attired waiter; Clemmons, an entrée of Medallion of Lobster with mushrooms, and me a simple Swiss cheese with Baked Ham on Rye with Cole Slaw, I once again brought our conversation back to the investigation.

"Did you specifically request that the prop master watch the 'extras' on the set?"

"Yes. It was brought to my attention by my staff that some of them were not handling their weapons convincingly." He took a sip of his white Bordeaux, a limited reserve, no less. This guy flaunted dough like a peacock's tail feathers. I stuck with something I could afford: water. He continued, "We had a quick meeting on the set and decided that Soames should supervise the action."

That sounded plausible, so I moved on to another issue.

"Who cast Miss Geary?"

"I don't know. I suspect one of my staff."

"You don't do the casting yourself?"

"Only the major roles. Miss Geary's was considered a 'bit'. She was playing a field nurse with two, maybe three lines of dialogue."

"Did you know Miss Geary personally?"

"Not personally, just professionally," he replied. "She has worked on several of my pictures in minor roles."

"So you wouldn't have any thoughts on who would like to see her dead?"

"I'm afraid not."

"What about the 'extra', Betty Jean?"

"Same answer," he replied shortly.

"Were you aware that Miss Hyland was being threatened?"

"Sorry, same answer." This guy was starting to sound like a parrot.

I decided it was time to go for the big question. His reaction to this was what I was most curious about.

"Did you lose a script recently?"

Bingo. He paled slightly, his fork skewered with a piece of lobster pausing momentarily on the way to his mouth. "Yes, but how did you know?"

"Just did a little digging." I replied vaguely, with the aim of steering the conversation away from fingering Rita. After all, she seemed like a nice girl, although I use "nice" not in the strictest terms, and I'd hate to see her lose a job because of me.

After he regained his composure, he mumbled, "Yeah, well, I might have misplaced it or something."

"And you don't think it was stolen?" I pressed.

"It could have been… I don't know." He made a show of patting his mouth with a cloth napkin, an unsuccessful attempt to cover his nervousness. "Why is this so important?"

"Because I suspect that the letters cut from it were used in a threatening note to my client, Miss Hyland."

This revelation took him utterly by surprise… and I knew then that I had him just as equally skewered as the lobster he had formerly on his fork!

I guess it seemed a little cold hearted on my part, harassing the guy paying for my meal. But let's face it, in this dog eat dog world, sometimes it doesn't pay to have scruples. I continued to lean on him further, but only got an admission that he wasn't sure how the script had disappeared, and swore he knew nothing about the threatening letter. Quite honestly I wasn't buying it, but decided for practical reasons to release the thumb screws, at least for the present. I mean, if he decided to storm off I might get stuck with the bill, and I wasn't up to washing dishes.

After lunch I was driven back to the studio. The atmosphere during the ride was tense, and we talked little. After dropping me at the main gate I searched out a phone, finally locating one in a booth at a corner drugstore. I slipped a nickel into the slot and dialed Red's office. I was lucky. He was in.

"Thomas." He seemed surprised to hear from me. "How'd ya know dat I would be working on a Saturday?"

"A zebra doesn't change its stripes, Red. You're a workaholic. I know your routine. We worked together once, right?"

"So we did… so we did…," he mumbled with some amusement. "And what, may I ask, is da purpose of this ill-timed interruption."

I caught him up on what I had learned, including the obviously calculated mishap in the property warehouse, and then asked how his end of the investigation was preceding.

"Look," he answered with a hint of exasperation, "I'm a detective, not a leprechaun. Da wheels of justice may still turn, but da rest of da world takes da weekend off!"

He then went on to explain that he didn't expect too many answers until, at the earliest, the middle of next week.

"Both 'Ballistics' and da crime lab hadn't time to begin work on da evidence Friday, and no one's around because of da weekend. Da bank is also closed, so my inquiries will have to wait until Monday. And I've given da book to Mary after it was 'dusted,' but it's too early to expect anything from her. No," he exclaimed with mild irritation, "it seems you're da only one making progress so far!"

"Well, that progress is certainly making someone nervous," I added thoughtfully.

"I'd keep my guard up if I were you," he added by way of warning. "That little incident in da prop warehouse reminds me of a saying I once heard from a wise Irish philosopher." I asked him what it was, and he quoted, "The closer you get to da truth, the more likely you are to raise the ire of your enemy,' or in other words, watch yar backside!"

"And what wise, Irish philosopher told you that?" I asked suspiciously.

"Me," he replied simply.

With these wise words still ringing in my ears, I decided to make a quick visit to my office. As I got into the elevator, the operator seemed surprised to see me. He told me that I had a visitor.

"He acted like he had an appointment, so I took him up. I thought that you were in your office." He closed the doors to the cage and pulled the lever which started our ascent.

"How long ago was that?" I asked, feeling oddly on edge.

"About half an hour ago," he replied, " and he hasn't come down since."

"What did he look like?"

"I couldn't really say." He then added, "Though he must have ice water for blood… the way he was bundled up and all!"

As we reached our floor, I immediately slipped out of my shoes and carefully tip-toed my way down the linoleum passageway while cautiously removing the Colt from its holster, and holding it at the ready by my side. Although I wasn't the type to wave firearms around needlessly, I wasn't about to repeat the same error I made at Betty Jean's apartment.

In reaching my office I could see that a light was lit inside. It reflected through the frosted glass pane of the door and transom. I reached slowly with my left hand for the knob, noting the minute scratches near the lock as I did so. It had obviously been picked. Carefully, I started turning it, angling my body off to one side and raising my gun. I wanted to present the least amount of target I could for my visitor and any weapon that he may have pointed in my direction. I started counting down from three and then kicked the door open with so much force that I thought it might come off its hinges. I was fast, but not fast enough, because the moment the door started swinging open the light was quickly extinguished. I stared into the darkness half expecting to be greeted by the flash of a muzzle, but was hailed instead, "Whoa, take it easy, Mister; I just came here to talk!"

"Go ahead," I said, my gun still pointed into the darkness.

"Do you mind losing the heater? You're making me nervous."

"I'll put it away *if* and *when* I like what I hear!" Then I ordered, "Turn on the light slowly and then open the blinds!"

He did, and it came as no surprise when the room was finally bathed in light that I was staring face to face with our mystery man, red scarf and all. However, what did astound me was, now that I was finally able to get a good look at him, he seemed oddly familiar. Like I'd seen him somewhere before, but couldn't exactly place when or where.

8

INTUITION OF DEATH

I don't take kindly to people who feel they can do whatever they want at the expense of my privacy. Locks are on the door for a reason. If you cross that threshold without being invited you're taking your chances. Trespassers tick me off. You touch my stuff, expect to pay the consequences. If you're wondering how I might react, let me paint this picture. A juicy, marrow-filled bone, and a ravenous bulldog. Now try and separate them!

He was standing by my desk. I ordered him to raise his hands slowly, and as he was staring at the business end of my gun, he hadn't any other choice but to obey. I walked over and carefully started frisking him.

"You got a name?" I asked while patting him down.

"I always figured names were for cemeteries," he replied. "However, you can call me John Smith."

"And I take it this is Pocahontas!" I remarked from the corner of my mouth, as I removed the automatic from his waistband.

He shrugged. "The streets aren't safe these days."

There didn't seem to be any other weapons, so I told him to take a seat. As he did so I made a mental note of his appearance: about 35; round face; hazel eyes; flat nose, probably broken; and black hair, most likely dyed.

"We meet somewhere before?"

He just looked at me and grinned. After a long pause I added, "Guess it might have been on a Post Office wall."

I don't think he found that funny.

"I didn't come here to be insulted!"

"So, what did you come for?"

I replaced the .45 back into my holster and positioned myself in a chair between him and the exit.

"Did you see the morning papers?" he asked, his voice rising in anger. "They're blaming me for these murders!"

"As I recall," I corrected evenly, "they stated that you were… and I quote, 'A person of interest.'"

"You know that's press talk. What they're really saying is that I'm responsible for the murders!"

"OK. We could argue semantics, but for the sake of this discussion let's agree that you are suspected. What's not to say that you didn't commit them?"

He looked around my office and spotted the whis-key bottle and glasses on top of my filing cabinet. He licked his lips and indicated them, "Do you mind?"

I did, but it gave me an idea. I told him to help him-self, and watched him carefully as he did, not relaxing until he once again took his seat.

"I'd change bootleggers," he remarked after taking a sip.

"Sorry. If I knew you were coming I would have bro-ken out the good stuff!" I rubbed my chin. "And speak-ing of this visit… what's the idea of breaking into my office?"

"Look, I'm desperate… I need to talk… and I have no place to go. It ain't safe for me out there. I'd figured to bunk here until you showed. I know you can help me."

"In what way?"

"Get the police off my back," he pleaded. "You know that I'm innocent!"

"I do?"

"You saw me enter William's apartment! I caught a glimpse of you watching. You witnessed me strug-gling with her killer." He suddenly became more fran-tic. "Look, I most likely saved your life. Who do you think got on the horn and alerted the police to your situation?"

"All right," I said, trying to calm him. "Let's say that you aren't guilty of Miss Williams' murder…what's not to say that you didn't kill Geary?"

"Because I was at the studio at her request. We were friends. She felt uncomfortable…threatened. She said she would feel safer if I hung around to keep an eye on things. I wasn't there to kill her, but to protect her."

"Considering the outcome," I commented dryly, "you need more practice in that department!"

"As long as we're keeping score, you haven't done too well yourself," he shot back. That stung; unfortunately he was right. I quickly changed the subject.

"How did you get into the studio? I checked with the guard and he hadn't recalled seeing you."

"Come on, Sherlock, we didn't want to advertise… and for reasons I'm not about to explain, I also wanted to keep my anonymity. That studio isn't all that secure. Vicki, Miss Geary to you, just let me in through the back gate."

Well, that solved one mystery. I decided to move in a different direction.

"You said she felt afraid. Did she mention receiving any threatening notes?"

"Not that I know of," he replied, taking a sip from his glass. "Again, you'll have to be satisfied with what I give you. If I'm not specific when it comes to details there's a reason. But let it be enough that she felt she was in danger."

"What about the Williams girl? You wrestled with her murderer. You must know his identity. Who was he?"

"It was too dark," he stated simply. "I didn't see his face."

He was lying, and not really doing a very good job of it. And furthermore, I don't think he cared if I bought it or not.

"Look," I stated pointedly. "If you're not frank with me, I may not be able to help you. All I'm looking for is a motive and a name."

"Forget the motive, and the name," he fired back. "I have my own plans for dealing with *that* problem, but I won't be able to accomplish it with the police on my back. Do we have a deal or not?"

I wanted to ask him what the hell he was talking about, but I knew it would get me nowhere. Instead I stated, "It all depends on whether I like what I hear. You answer my questions and I'm convinced you're innocent of the crimes…I might help you."

He thought a second, taking another slow, thoughtful sip from the glass. "I'd prefer a more definite answer," he finally concluded. "But I'll take my chances. Go ahead."

"Let's start with this," I began. "Could you relate to me as precisely as possible your movements at the studio the day of the murder?"

"I was standing, most of the time, over by the generator, just opposite the set and far enough away to get an overall view of the production, and specifically Vicki."

"Then, if you were focused on Miss Geary, you should be able to describe to me exactly what went on around her just prior to her being shot."

"Sure." He thought for a moment, and then continued, "she was standing and talking to Hyland, Williams and that hairdresser…"

"Wait a moment!" I interrupted. "You mean Fran Adams was part of the group?"

"Yeah, she kept going back and forth between them and her duties on the set." He paused to see if I was satisfied with his answer, and then continued, "Anyway, I saw Vicki walk away toward where they had the coffee and she sort of gave me the eye to follow her, which I did. We met partway and she pulled me aside to say that she was getting this weird feeling that something bad was going to happen. She didn't know what or when, but she asked me to keep on my toes."

"And then what?"

"Well, she told me to stall for a few minutes, until she got her coffee…"

"Hold it," I broke in again. "Did you say that she got a cup of coffee?" He nodded. "I was told by a witness that she didn't."

"Then they were wrong," he responded unequivocally and then resumed his narrative. "I waited about five, maybe ten minutes… and when I checked back to where she had been standing, I noticed that she was now sitting in a chair and being fussed over by the other ladies. The Hyland dame, I believe, was just walking away to get something or another…I believe it was a glass of water."

"Did Miss Hyland go on her own, or did someone send her?" I asked quickly.

"I couldn't say. I just happened to overhear the Williams girl say that Hyland was going to get water." He returned to his narrative. "Anyhow, it was Vicki's and my agreement that I was to keep as low a profile as possible— at least concerning our association, so I decided to continue to watch from a distance."

"And from where at this point?"

"I can't say for certain." He then added, "Maybe the same place as before."

"Are you aware that someone saw you over by the Property Boxes? That's significant, because it's only fair to tell you that's where we believe the shot was fired."

"I may have wandered over in that direction earlier, but I can swear on my mother's grave that I was nowhere near there at the time of the murder!"

"OK, let's say that's true," I countered. "So, what were you doing there earlier?"

"I was following the hairdresser."

"How's that?" The statement caught me by surprise.

"When I noticed Vicki being fussed over in the chair, I also saw the hairdresser picking up her fallen coffee cup. She was acting really suspicious… enough so that I decided to follow and see what she was up to. She had headed toward the boxes, but by the time I had gotten there she had disappeared. As I started back, trying to determine my next move, I saw Vicki fall forward onto the floor…"

"And then by all reports you ran." I chided, in the hopes that the jab might cause him to slip.

"Yeah, I did," he returned honestly, "but not for what you think. I didn't know that she had been shot… I figured maybe poison or drugs. I mean there was so much gunfire and noise coming from the set… who would have known? In any case, no sooner had that occurred, than I thought I caught sight of the hairdresser heading toward the sound stages. I took off after her, but was either mistaken or she had deliberately given me the slip, because when I got there she was gone, and then I spotted her back on the set. Some gaffers were shouting that Vicki had been killed, so I decided that it was time to make a quick exit. Not the wisest move in hindsight, but the only one I had left."

I thought otherwise. "You could have stayed and gotten interviewed with the rest of the witnesses."

"I'm allergic to badges, if you know what I mean."

"So what did you do next?" I asked after a considerable pause.

"Wandered a bit until it started to get dark and then decided to go to Vicki's apartment. I knew I was taking a chance, but I had to get my hands on something she was holding for me."

My attention level rose a couple of notches. He took another sip of my booze as I waited impatiently for him to continue.

"This stuff sort of grows on you," he commented, wiping his chin with the back of his hand.

"You were saying?" I reminded.

"I arrived at the apartment about the same time as you did. I was across the street when you entered the garden. I decided to hang out there and wait until you returned. However when about forty minutes passed, I got curious. I slipped into the garden and hid for a few minutes, and then made my way up the stairs to the front door. There were some strange noises coming from inside… strange enough to tell me that I needed to take some immediate action… and, well you know the rest."

"Everything, except what it was that Miss Geary was holding for you." I stated, steering him back to the subject that had really peaked my interest.

"A leather book… black… with a lock." He roughly tried to simulate its dimensions with his hands. "About so big. Why, have you seen it?"

"Perhaps," I replied carefully. "What is it?"

"Well, let's call it my insurance policy."

"Could you speak a little plainer?" I asked, but could pretty much anticipate the answer.

"I could, but I won't. However, the question still stands, did you see it?"

"Perhaps," I repeated, being just as obstinate as he was. After all, two could play at this game!

9

THE INSURANCE POLICY

There's nothing more effective to put a man off his stride than the seductive wiles of the opposite sex. A glimpse of thigh or a revealing neckline could cause more damage to a male's concentration than if his head had been cut off at the neck. If you don't believe me ask Samson; he got more than a haircut from that scheming Delilah!

He said it was his 'Insurance policy'? Now that intrigued me. He continued, "If you happen to have that item, I would be willing to pay."

"I might be able to get my hands on it… for the right price," I responded, figuring that if I played along I might learn something.

"Then I take it you don't have it at the moment?" he asked, his eyes suddenly narrowing.

"I think you already know the answer to that question..." I replied, noticing that some of the items in my office had been moved from their usual place.

One would never guess it looking at me, but I have a thing about order. I have a certain way that I organize my belongings. Books arranged in alphabetical order, blotter placed squarely on the desk, paper weight exactly off to one side... It was an obsession. Obviously my friend had been busy before my arrival.

I then added as an afterthought, "Unless you think that I'm carrying it on me, which incidentally I'm not. But, you're welcome to check."

"Naw, I figure you're leveling with me." He suddenly became panicked. "The cops don't have it, do they?"

"No," I lied. "Not yet."

What can I say; I'm a detective not a boy scout. Besides, I crossed my fingers when I said it. I continued, "Why is this book so important, anyway?"

"You don't worry about that... it doesn't concern you. Just get me the merchandise and there'll be some bucks in it..." He polished off the last drop of whiskey and added, "then you could afford some decent hooch." He leaned forward. "Now, can I count on you to keep the cops off my back?"

"It may be against my better judgment, but I'll talk to them." I then added quickly, "Although I can't guarantee the outcome."

He thought on this a second before responding, "Fair enough!"

There was a long pause and then I asked, "Since you're talking about keeping people off one's back… you wouldn't happen to know who might be tailing my client?" He shrugged his shoulder, so I pressed further, "He was hanging around this building last Thursday just after noon?"

He shrugged again and added, "I really don't know what you're talking about."

"Whoever it was, was dressed like you right down to the red scarf!"

I wasn't going to let him off the hook.

"Probably just another snappy dresser," he suggested with a silly grin. When he saw I wasn't amused, he quickly added, "Look, it wasn't me, I swear it. Now, do we have a deal regarding the book, or what?"

I handed him my card. "Here's my number. My home phone's on the back. Do you have a number where you can be reached when, *and if* I recover the said item?"

"As I mentioned earlier, I haven't quite figured that out yet. I need somewhere safe to hide." He indicated the office. "Is this place up for grabs?" He looked at me questioningly. After a long pause, he concluded, "naw, I didn't think so. And you don't look the type who'd consider putting me up at your place either." When I didn't respond again, he picked up his hat and headed for the door. Partway he stopped, and turned toward me. "I think you have something else of mine." He was referring to his automatic. I tossed it over to him. After replacing it in his waistband, he added, "I'll be in touch," and then, without so much as a backward glance, he walked out.

Immediately I ran to the filing cabinet and removed a pair of binoculars that I had tucked away there, and then, extinguishing all the lights, took a position to one side of my window. It had gotten dark while we had been talking, but there was enough light from the streetlamps to observe the detail on the street below. He hadn't appeared yet, so I did a quick survey along both sides of the boulevard, pausing only when I noticed his sedan, again parked directly across from the building almost in the same spot I'd seen it three days ago. However, there was something strange, because as I was observing the window by the driver's side I could almost swear that I saw the glow of a cigarette coming from inside. This was further confirmed when my 'Mister Smith' stepped out onto the sidewalk. Instead of heading across the street for the car as I expected, he instead turned left and moved with a rapid gait up the sidewalk and disappeared around the corner. Seconds later the headlights of the car switched on and pulled out of the space moving along the boulevard in the same direction. My binoculars allowed me to see part of the plate, they were commercial. I dropped the binoculars onto the desk and ran for the hall. I didn't bother making for the elevator, but took the steps instead. I leapt more than ran down the five flights and reached the front of the building in just under three minutes. I immediately made for the corner, but upon arrival found neither Smith nor the automobile. Both had vanished.

Upon returning to my office I dropped into a chair. 'This had been one hell of a couple of days', I thought, sliding my hat back and wincing as the sweat band rubbed against the sore on my scalp. Running my hand along my chin, I studied the situation, contemplating my next move. I glanced over at the whiskey bottle and spotted Smith's dirty glass. Searching around the bottom drawer of my desk, I located a paper bag, which with the aid of a handkerchief, I placed both the bottle and glass inside. I looked at my watch. It was too late to call Red at his office, and I wasn't about to disturb him at home. It could wait. But I was certain that the prints which Smith left on its surface would be of interest, so I planned to ask him to dust it. I would also request a toxicology test be performed on Miss Geary, considering the story I just heard.

I reached into my coat pocket and removed my notebook. My client's telephone number was in it. I dialed it. Her butler answered and after a long pause she picked up the line:

"Hi, Logan, any luck yet?" she asked cheerfully. I detected a slight slur and suspected that she had been drinking. For a country under prohibition laws there sure seemed to be a lot of drinking going on…present company not excluded.

"Perhaps," I replied, feeling noncommittal.

"But, I'm curious. I can't wait until tomorrow," she persisted. "Did you find out anything about that note that was sent to me?"

"Only that it looks like it might have been put together using Jack Clemmons' script."

There was a pause on the other end, long enough to make me suspect that we might've been cut off. She finally replied, "You don't suspect Jack, do you?"

"Right now everyone's guilty in my book." I waited to see if she would respond, and when she didn't I continued, "However, anyone could have gotten hold of his script and used it. Still, I don't think it was Clemmons. I can't figure him stupid enough to use an item that could so easily be traced back to him."

"Then you still don't have any idea who actually sent it?"

"That's the long and short of it," I reconfirmed. "In any case, I'd like to talk to you tomorrow if that's possible?"

"Working on a Sunday. I sure have to commend you for your dedication." She paused for a second and I heard ice rattling in her glass on the other end. "Sure, why not. I am staying at my father's place in Bel Air... Say, one o'clock?"

"Sounds fine."

Before she hung up she put the butler on the phone who gave me directions to the place.

I knew the neighborhood. It spelled Class with a capital "C." That's why I opted for a cab instead of my usual public transportation. We passed west through Beverly Hills, to the exclusive Bel Air properties nestled like a golden goose egg amongst the surrounding hillsides. The place I sought out had a large iron gate guarded over by two stern looking stone lions. The property even had a name that bespoke of riches: "La casa de tesoro"- The Treasure House. My driver sounded his horn and a caretaker came out of an adjacent shed. He pulled open one of the massive gates and waved us through. The estate was atop a hill, and we followed a paved road that would eventually take us up to the front entrance.

As we drove the eight or so acres that fronted the main house, we passed a small garden of flowering shrubs, which soon opened onto a large expanse of manicured lawn shaded by tall date palms. The building's architecture reminded me of an Italian villa I'd once seen in a travel brochure. You know the one I mean; standing by some lake surrounded by ornate fountains and marble statues that would make the Vatican blush. An attendant ran over as we pulled to a stop and opened the door for me. I quickly paid the driver his fare and followed the man up to the entrance. As we stepped into the immense front hall, I was handed over to the butler, the same one I had talked to the night before. I'd recognized his voice. He asked me to follow him.

As he escorted me through the length of the house, I caught a quick glimpse of the various rooms. They were impressive, but cold as a museum. We eventually arrived at a set of French doors that led onto the back veranda. The butler indicated a descending staircase that was located at the far end. He said that Miss Hyland asked that I join her at the pool and then indicated that I should go on without him.

I followed the stairs down a steep hill that led to a wide cement patio surrounding a large Olympic-sized swimming pool. My client was doing laps when I arrived. She must have seen me, because she started for my side of the pool as I walked up. She rested both her arms along the edge and squinted in my direction, as my back was to the sun. Her blue eyes were red from the chlorine.

"Logan?" she asked in between breaths.

"Yeah."

"What do you think of my humble abode?"

"Humble isn't exactly the word I would choose for it!"

She started to pull herself out and I offered her a towel, which I removed from a nearby deck chair. She pulled the white bathing cap from her head and shook her short golden curls free.

As she started to dry off I couldn't help but notice the black bathing suit she was wearing. Well, perhaps the figure under it. Daddy's girl was indeed all grown up today!

"Admiring the view?" she asked playfully.

"You do get a nice view of the valley from here," I replied, nodding to the vista. I was feigning ignorance, but I don't think she was buying it.

"Do my back?" she asked with a devilish glint in her eye, as she handed me her towel and twisted around. I ran the towel in slow tight circles across her shoulders and along her spine, both of which were exposed by the suit's cut; and as I dried her, I noticed that she kept making these sounds like a contented cat being stroked by its master's hand.

"You're giving me goose bumps," she giggled, pointing to the hairs on her forearm that were now standing on end.

I knew it was all a tease, the question was to what end? After a few seconds of this operation she looked over her shoulder and gave me a mischievous little grin. I handed her back the towel and told her to let the sun do the rest.

She put on a white terry cloth bathrobe, making sure that it hung seductively below one shoulder, and stretched her tall, lithe frame out onto a wooden deck chair. I took a seat in an Adirondack chair close by.

"Care for a drink?" she purred, while placing her evenly bronzed arm into a large straw bag, fishing around for a pair of dark sunglasses. "Our man makes a mean 'Mint Julep'!"

I was just about to accept when the crack of a shotgun rang out, disturbing our peaceful interlude.

10

A BULLET TOO CLOSE
FOR COMFORT

Nothing is more demoralizing to the soul than being set up as a clay pigeon. To be someone's target isn't exactly my goal in life. It's not like I get up every morning, look in the mirror and say, "Gee Logan, wouldn't it be great to get shot at today. No. If anybody's going to be doing the shooting, you can damn well be sure that it is going to be me!

The shot echoed through the valley. I'd reached for the Colt, but halted when I saw the expression of amusement on Hyland's face.

"Are you getting jumpy, Mister Logan?"

"No, just cautious, Miss Hyland," I answered, removing my hand from underneath my suit jacket.

"You can drop the formality," she smiled sweetly. "After that intimate moment we just shared, I think you earned the right to call me Mattie."

I didn't think drying her back off with a towel was considered being intimate. More like civic duty. But, let her dream on.

"Well, Mattie, considering two dead women and a crack on the skull, I figure caution should be the order of the day." I then added with emphasis, "Now, what the Hell was that?"

"We've been having gopher problems," she explained simply. "This has been going on for days. Our gardener prefers bullets to poison." She picked up what I could only describe as a small school bell from the wooden table next to her and rang it. It summoned the butler who appeared at our side in a matter of minutes. "We'll have two Juleps, Harold," she ordered, and then looking at me asked, "Tart or sweet?" I told her tart.

"Now, about those questions..." I began after he had left to prepare our drinks.

She held up a hand. "First I want to apologize for my manners Friday. I was rude and I want to say how sorry I am. I was really scared and mixed up. I know that's no excuse, but it was the reason for my outburst."

"Sure, kid," I answered. "I think it caught us all by surprise."

"Thanks." She seemed satisfied with my response. "Now that we have that behind us... what do you want to know?" She leaned forward in a manner that told me I now had her complete attention.

"First off, from your perspective, could you relate what went on around you prior to the murder?"

"I was talking to the three ladies…Miss Geary, Miss Williams, and Fran Adams. We were discussing nothing really important, just a bunch of 'chit chat'. And then Geary started complaining that she was feeling kind of dizzy…"

"Did you notice, was this before or after she drank her coffee?" I interrupted.

"Oh, that's right," she answered suddenly remembering. "She did go off and get some coffee." She thought for a second and then replied, "You know, I can't be sure…"

"Try," I asked, urging her on. "This could be important."

She thought again, and then responded vaguely, "I really don't know… but it might have been after."

I told her to continue.

"Well, we sat her down in my chair and I ran off to get some water…"

"Sorry to interrupt again," I said, "but did anyone suggest that you do that?"

"Not that I recall. I think it was just one of those spontaneous decisions."

"Are you sure?" I pressed. "One of my witnesses suggested that it could have been the director."

"No, definitely not!"

"How could you be so sure?"

"He was over by the camera. I don't think he was even aware of the situation." She suddenly became flustered. "Logan, I still don't understand. Why all the questions? Someone took me for Geary. It's as simple as that!"

"The one thing I learned in this business is that it is never that simple."

"Then how do you explain the note?"

"I can't," I replied shortly. "But let's suppose you weren't the only person to receive one."

"Do you think she got one also?"

"I was told that she hadn't. But I'm not altogether sure I can trust my source yet."

"But you have to admit," she argued, "that Geary and I look the same from behind!"

"So do a hundred other blondes in this town."

Actually that wasn't a good answer on my part. She was making a valid point. The size, shape, haircut, and hair coloring even fooled me that day, but nevertheless it still just didn't feel right.

"But for argument sake," I continued, "let's say that Geary was the intended victim…"

"I still think you're wrong, Logan," she interrupted.

"Look, just trust me on this…" I urged. "Just play along and answer my questions." Reluctantly she nodded, and I returned to my previous line of inquiry:

"After Geary started feeling ill, did anyone in the group take charge of the situation?"

"I don't know exactly what you're looking for, Logan?" she replied. "But, if I were to say anyone, I guess I could say that Fran Adams did try to take charge when it happened."

"Did you see her remove Geary's coffee cup after she had dropped it?"

"I don't believe so."

"Then I guess you wouldn't have noticed where she wandered off to afterwards?"

"Not really," she replied again with evident frustration. "I wasn't particularly paying attention to her at the time. I was more concerned about Geary!"

"Perhaps you were getting water?"

"That's possible."

"And when you did, did you see or pass anyone along the way?"

"Well, now that you mention it," she replied, as if suddenly recalling, "Fran did run past me… and I think I saw that strange man with the scarf as well. *And what about him?* If you ask me he's obviously the killer!"

"And I have reasons to suspect not."

She seemed surprised at the confidence of my statement.

"When you saw the man with the scarf, " I continued, "what direction was he coming from?"

"I think he was walking toward the set."

"Toward the set? Are you sure?"

She thought again, "Yes. I believe so."

"And then what?"

"I got the water from Craft Services and just as I returned, saw Geary fall from the chair. I thought she might have fainted, but…" Her voice trailed off, and she momentarily stared down at the ground biting her lip.

The butler showed up with the drinks and I sipped mine slowly, studying her face. I just couldn't make her out. And although I couldn't see her eyes behind the dark glasses, I sensed she was appraising me as well.

"What about Williams" she asked after a long pause. "I was surprised to read about it in the paper. Do you think her murder is somehow connected to Geary's?"

I wanted to say that you'd have to be pretty dim not to see the connection, but didn't, because I suspected that what she was really after was my personal views on the matter.

"I think she was killed because of something she saw or heard that day," I replied; conveniently leaving out any mention of the black book. I decided to keep that detail under wraps for the moment.

"What do you think could've been the connection?"

"I wish I could say," I replied truthfully. "I'm afraid she took that secret to the grave."

"How was she killed?" Here I could tell that she was curious, but at the same time didn't really want to hear the details. Nonetheless, I wasn't going to sugar coat it.

"Her neck was broken, and she was beaten brutally. There were welts and bruises all over her body."

She paled and bit her lip again. After a pause she lamented:

"Oh, God, that poor child. I didn't realize!"

After witnessing her reaction, I felt guilty at my bluntness, and quickly changed the subject.

"How well did you know Geary?"

"Not very," she replied after a fashion. I had to ask the question twice, because her mind was obviously still on Williams. "She worked on a few of our productions periodically over the last few months."

"Do you think she might be mixed up in blackmail?"

Here again she seemed surprised, but before she could answer her head rose sharply and I noticed that she was squinting.

Something over my shoulder had caught her attention, and I turned to see what it was. A man, perhaps in his late sixties, was walking toward us. He was nicely dressed and carried himself in a manner that suggested he was used to garnering respect. She leaned over and whispered urgently into my ear, "Who is that?" I described the gentleman briefly. This seemed to alarm her even more. "That's Daddy. He knows about the murder, but please don't say anything about the note. I don't want to worry him!"

He came over and immediately shook my hand. His grip was dry and firm. "I know what you've been thinking," he began, the statement catching me by surprise. "You wondered how much milk I'd needed to sell to live in such luxury." I stared at him, desperately seeking an answer; luckily he saved me the effort. "A whole damn lot!" he laughed. Then added seriously, "I'm sure glad you're looking into this business at the studio. Really nasty stuff! Poor girl; and I feel bad for her parents as well. Sorry my little girl had to get mixed up in it though. Hope you don't suspect her of anything?"

"It's a terrible situation," I responded tactfully, "but regarding your daughter, it's just normal procedure to collect statements from witnesses."

"Hope the force pays you overtime for working weekends."

"Well actually, I'm a private investigator…"

I wasn't able to complete my sentence because a loud crack from the gardener's shotgun suddenly filled the air and a chunk of cement exploded in a puff of dust just feet from where we were standing. The pellets had hit the edge of the patio and we all scrambled to find cover, hunkering down with baited breath, as we waited in anticipation for another shot to follow. I had my gun out and was carefully surveying the horizon, while simultaneously running through my mind the details of what had just happened.

The sound was much louder than before, and it seemed to come from an area slightly closer. A strange echo had followed, which made it hard to guess the direction.

After several long minutes a man carrying a shotgun suddenly appeared on the edge of the patio.

"Are you alright? "he asked, obviously shaken by the incident.

"You fool," cried the elder Hyland rising from behind a table. "You could have killed us!"

"I can't be sure what happened, sir," he countered, perspiration evident on his brow. "I was just shooting at a gopher up on that hill…" he indicated a general direction waving his hand "… and I'm sure I was aiming low when I saw you all dive for cover. I can't possibly see how the pellets could have gone so far afield!"

"Well, obviously they did!" Hyland exclaimed, his face growing redder. "There will be no more of that… *from now on* use poison or traps!" The gardener's complexion had turned ashen, and with head bowed low, he made a hasty retreat toward the house. As he got out of earshot, Hyland commented to us that the man was simply being careless.

I wasn't so convinced, and started to say so when I glanced over his shoulder at his daughter, who put a finger quickly up to her lips and shook her head warning me to be quiet. It was evident that she was scared, but not frightened enough to let on anything to her father.

"I could use a drink." Mr. Hyland said, breathing a sigh of relief. "You kids want to freshen yours up?"

"No thanks," I replied, replacing the gun back into my holster. "I think I've concluded my business with your daughter for today."

"Well, I hope this little episode didn't scare you off," he exclaimed, trying to sound jovial. "We don't usually shoot at our guests until the second visit. But look, you come back again anytime. I'd love to show you around the estate."

After shaking my hand and apologizing a second time for the unfortunate incident, he headed back toward the house.

"Look," I said to the girl, once her father had walked away, "that sounded like two shots being fired! I think your gardener was right." I took her by the arm. She was shivering, and the goose bumps standing out on her skin were certainly not due to the 80-degree weather. "I need to look around." I urged, shaking her gently for emphasis.

"OK," she conceded, "but don't be too obvious and do it quickly! My father can put two and two together… and I don't want to alarm him!"

I agreed.

"Perhaps I was wrong and you were right," I explained as I took her by the hand and led her quickly toward the veranda. "Someone warned you in that note to keep your mouth shut…and it could well be that they're making good on that promise!"

After seeing her safely into the house, and making her promise to stay clear of any of the windows, I doubled back and methodically crisscrossed the grounds. It was a wooded area, full of tall Eucalyptus trees, thick bushes, and deep gullies, which I soon realized would prove too difficult to search effectively in the time that

I was allowed. I therefore made directly for the perimeter wall, which was tall, but not impossible to climb. Exerting a moderate amount of energy anyone could scale its rough stone surface and gain easy access to the property. I canvassed a fairly long stretch of it, pausing only at a section where I thought some creeping vines looked displaced. Upon closer examination, however, I dismissed it, because the ground at its base seemed relatively undisturbed. I eventually gave up my search, deeming it fruitless, and walked resignedly back to the front gate.

Somewhere a radio was blaring one of Aimee McPherson's fiery Sunday sermons. It was coming from the gatekeeper's shed.

Upon entering, I asked the man if I could use his phone to call for a cab.

"Sure, go ahead. It's on the desk." As I picked up the receiver I glanced over in his direction and noticed that he seemed confused. Sensing that he had something troubling on his mind I asked, "Is there a problem?"

"Well," he said scratching his head, "I was just wondering why you didn't leave with your friend?"

"How's that?" I asked, placing the receiver slowly back down on its cradle.

"Your friend?" he replied, obviously thinking that I would understand the inference. When I didn't respond he added, "You did see him up at the house, didn't you?"

"No," I answered simply.

"He came about five... maybe ten minutes after you arrived and said he was here to give you a ride back to your office... when you finished your interview with Miss Hyland, of course. I told him he could park the car up at the house, but he said he preferred to leave it out on the street. He said something about the crank case leaking oil..."

"Did you see this man leave?" I asked, interrupting him with some urgency.

"Yes. He took off just about five minutes ago. He said you were planning to stay around for supper and didn't need him."

"What was he driving?" I asked quickly.

"Dark colored sedan."

"Anything else?"

"I'm afraid that's all I remember," he replied vaguely.

"Plates? Commercial?" I further prompted.

"I couldn't say."

"And what did this friend of mine look like?"

"Strange," he replied shaking his head. "He was dressed like it was twenty below... and now that you've asked, I don't think I could give you a description of his face...he was pretty covered up."

"When you let him in was he carrying anything?"

"No, sir, I believe not. However he did have a golf bag when he left."

"And you didn't find that strange?" I asked. "Do you know someone just took a shot at us?

"Please sir, don't say anything to Mr. Hyland. I need this job… I have a family… and the times are so tough right now!"

I held up my hand.

"Don't worry, friend, it'll be our little secret. However, in the future, for your employer's sake, I'd be a little more selective in who you let through these gates." I handed him my card. "And if you see this fellow again, you keep him out and call me at this number."

He nodded his consent like a scolded school boy, and slipped the card into his breast pocket. I hated to sound like an nasty old schoolmaster from Dickens, but this guy's lack of vigilance could have resulted in someone's death…which included, yours truly!

11

DECIPHERING THE CODE

*Have you ever looked into one of those
kaleidoscopes as a kid? The more you twisted
the tube, the greater number of different
patterns it formed. I can't help but make the
same comparison between it and this case.
Just as you start to see it one way, a slight
turn and it seems like something else.*

As with spots on a leopard, the gatekeeper's description of my 'friend' resembled Smith to
a 'T.' The golf bag explained how he'd concealed the weapon, and the fact that the gatekeeper
hadn't seen him carrying it into the estate didn't trouble me in the least, because it would have been easy for
Smith to toss the bag over the wall, and then retrieve
it on the other end. And although it would have been
just as easy to reverse the process after the shooting,

perhaps haste was the reason he'd just carried it out through the gate.

The question is, I pondered on the cab ride back to my apartment, was this indeed the real 'Mr. Smith' or some imposter? It didn't take a Bulldog Drummond to figure out that a 'ringer' could be a possibility considering what I had witnessed from my office window the previous night. And regarding this appearance, I found it strange that he hadn't bypassed the gate altogether and climbed the wall… unless the idea was that he was supposed to be seen. That was telling in itself. And who was the intended target… Miss Hyland or myself? The more I tried to reason this out the more evident it was that this case had more twists to it than a stick of licorice.

Considering all that occurred that day I was able to get a good night's sleep, and was up all the earlier Monday morning. My first stop was going to be the Homicide Division at H.Q., however, just as I started to head out the door my phone rang. It was Mr. Smith.

"You got my package yet?" he directly asked, skipping the usual formalities.

"It's only been a day," I replied simply. "I take it you found a hole to crawl in."

"Now that's not very nice, considering how helpful I've been and all."

"I wouldn't call squirting metal at me being helpful."

"I'm afraid I don't follow?"

"You didn't take a shot at me yesterday?"

"No." He sounded surprised. "I was too busy watching my own back… and why would I want to stiff you anyway? I need you to deliver my package. And what was the idea of putting a tail on me? I spent a good part of the night trying to dodge it."

"It wasn't me," I replied briefly.

"Well, it wasn't me taking a shot at you either!"

"OK. I believe you. For reasons I don't want to go into I believe someone's playing us one against the other. You have a number where I can reach you? When I get my hands on the package, that is."

"Like before, I'll be in touch with you. If not by phone, I'll catch you at your place on Bunker Hill."

Surprised I asked, "Where did you get that piece of information?"

"Not much of a Sherlock, are you? I got it off of that P.I. license you got framed in your office. I saw it while cooling my heels waiting for you the other night."

More like 'snooping' I thought to myself. In any case, you certainly had to hand it to him, if nothing else, he was resourceful.

I placed the brown bag on top of Red's desk and dropped into the chair opposite him. He carefully undid the folds and peeked inside.

"What, da ya bringing the boys and me some donuts?" He spotted the bottle. "Ah, bless ya me boy!"

"I need it analyzed." I then added quickly with a smile, "Not the contents. But, I'd like the bottle and the glass dusted, and the owner's prints identified."

I then told him briefly about my visit from Mr. Smith and explained why I thought it might be advisable to look elsewhere for our murderer.

"I think someone's going to great lengths to pin these crimes on Smith," I suggested. "The question is, why?"

"So ya think he's innocent?"

"Of the murders, yes. However, he does tie in somewhere, and that's why learning his identity might turn up something useful."

One of his detectives came over with a mug of steaming hot coffee and placed it in front of me.

"I figured ya didn't have time for breakfast," Red explained, and offered me a slice of his Irish bread. "My woman made it last night. I remember how much ya used to enjoy it!"

That reminded me.

"Red, I think you might want to ask the coroner to run a toxicology test on Geary's body…both blood and stomach contents. From what Smith told me last night, there's a good chance that she was drugged prior to the murder."

"I'll do me best," Red replied, his mouth full. He washed it down with some coffee and continued, "But this may take some time. Da boys in the lab are already screaming about da workload. Ya know there are still just two of dem. They have hopes of getting a third person from da university soon!"

"Well, send it out to an outside lab if you have to. I think this is important."

"What I don't understand," he asked, taking another bite, "is what advantage would there be of drugging da woman if you plan to shoot her?"

"I have some ideas on that," I replied, sampling the bread for the first time. It was just as good as I'd remembered it. After swallowing a mouthful of coffee, I continued, "But I think it's really too early to draw any conclusions, especially without knowing all the facts. Let's prove that she was drugged first, and then move on from there."

"How did it go with yar client? Did ya learn anything new?"

"Not directly."

"How 'bout indirectly?"

"A lot. But there again, I don't want to put the cart before the horse. I'll need more proof before drawing any conclusions. However, one thing is for certain; our killer is getting desperate. He took a shot at me at Hyland's estate."

I thought Red was going to spit his bread out.

"How's dat, Thomas?"

"I think he's starting to feel the heat," I explained further, and then detailed quickly what had occurred.

I concluded with the observation that, "This last attempt was both clumsy and risky on his part, which makes me think he's starting to panic."

Having completed the information from my end, I then asked, "How's Mary doing with the book?"

He looked over my shoulder and responded, "Ask her for yar self, me boy!"

Mary Kelly hadn't changed from the last time I saw her. A little pixie of a girl, with short copper red hair, large emerald green eyes, and a pert, upturned nose dusted with freckles.

"Hi, Logan," she greeted me with a slight giggle to her voice. "How's my favorite cop?"

"Ex-cop," I reminded her. "And to answer your question… desperate. How are you doing with the book?"

"I've made some progress. Do you want to hear?"

"Sure, what do you have?" I asked, as she laid the book and her notes onto the desk in front of us.

"To begin with," she stated, assuming the role of lecturer, "I spent a good deal of the weekend just puzzling over what I assume is a correct but very perplexing translation of the text. There has to be a key to decode it, but unfortunately I have yet to find it."

I must have looked disappointed, because she quickly added, "However, there are some details about it that are very telling." She opened the book and pointed to some figures. "These numbers are obvious, and the particular value on this page matches the amount on the bank receipt that you found lodged between the pages. Therefore, we can safely assume that it is in part some type of ledger. The pictograms are interesting too, and I believe that they represent words that do not have the equivalent in the shorthand being used…"

"Shorthand?" I asked, interrupting.

"Yes. It's a variation of the Anniversary Series of Gregg Shorthand, which is not based on the actual letters of a word, but is more phonetic." I guess I still looked puzzled, because she went on to explain, "Using the sounds of speech rather than its spelling."

I nodded and then asked, "So what did this short-hand tell you?"

"That's the problem. I don't know," she replied, looking both thoughtful and disappointed. "It seems like a foreign language… definitely not English, but not French, Italian, or German either."

Red took her notes and looked them over. After a moment his face broke into a wide grin and he chuck-led. We both must have looked at him startled, because he quickly explained, "Wat's da matter with you, me girl! Don't you recognize yar mother country's lingo." She shook her head, still not grasping his meaning, so he continued, "It's ancient Gaelic!"

"I was born in Hoboken," she reminded him.

"I've forgotten, ya poor girl." He gathered up her notes and handed them to her. "Take these down to St. Brendan's. Father McCarthy is well versed in da lan-guage. Ask him to translate it for us!" And with those orders she was whisked out the door.

Red walked over to his window carrying his coffee mug and looked out over the Los Angeles basin. After a moment he turned looking self-satisfied and stated, "Well, it looks like we've finally got something." He then became thoughtful. "But we still have far to go. I envy you…" he sighed. "You get to do da foot work and I'm stuck here waiting on da wheels of justice. I hate da red tape connected with this job, but I have to deal with it. Like now, I can't make a move with the bank until the legal department gets da proper paperwork together. I'm certain Geary's records will provide us with some answers, but we are stymied because of da legal issues."

"When did you make the request?" I asked.

"First thing this morning, but heavens know when they'll get to it!"

"Did you tell them it was a rush?"

"Are ya kiddin?" he replied. "That would give them an excuse to take twice as long. Ya know da boys in da legal department." He took a deep breath and let it out slowly. "So, what's on board for ya today?"

"Continue the investigation," I said shortly. "I have a lot planned, but whether I accomplish it all today depends on the availability of the individuals. Most of the people I need to question are at the studio, so at least I won't waste time wandering around. However, if I could work it in I would also like to question Geary's agent."

"And who do ya need to talk to at da studio?"

"Well considering that incident yesterday at Hyland's estate, I think it would be valuable to check in with the Transportation Department. That automobile has shown up several times now, and at each appearance Mr. Smith, or a likeness thereof, was associated with it. Maybe their records could shed some light on the matter."

"Good idea. What else?"

"Well, I haven't finished interviewing some of the major players yet. I still need to talk to Adams and Taylor. That reminds me. Do you mind if I use your telephone?"

He said no and I proceeded to dial the studio. The switchboard connected me directly to the production office. Rita was off, but I got to talk to another receptionist who identified herself as Lana. I told her who I was, and what it was that I was investigating, and then asked if it was possible to set up an appointment with either or both the assistant director and the hairdresser. She checked with Taylor who told her that he would work me in after one o'clock, but she reported that Fran Adams had not shown up for work yet.

"She's late," she informed me in a timid voice. "And she hasn't called in."

"Is this usual for her?" I asked.

"Not at all. She has always been very conscientious."

"When was she at work last?"

"I really can't say. I didn't work this last weekend," she replied. "You would have to ask somebody in her department. They might know."

"Connect me," I ordered. I waited for several minutes, and then eventually heard the phone ring on the other end. A woman identifying herself as Connie Wilson answered.

I immediately stated, "My name is Logan; I'm a private investigator looking into the Geary-Williams murders. I need to contact Miss Adams…"

"I'm sorry, but she hasn't checked in."

"I am aware of that," I answered. "Do you know when she worked last?"

"Friday."

"Did she indicate that she wouldn't be coming in today?"

"I don't believe so."

"And no one has seen or heard from her since?"

"Not as far as I know." She then added, "We've tried reaching her at home, but there's no answer."

"Will you be at the studio later?"

She said she was going out on location to cover for Adams, but should be back by noon. I told her I would stop by to talk with her.

"Twenty-four hours," Red reminded me as I hung up, and before I could even ask the question. "We can't act officially until da person is missing a full twenty-four hours after a report is made."

"The way things are moving, we may not have that much time."

"Nevertheless… And that brings us back to wat I was talking about earlier…red tape."

"OK," I said resignedly, "just one more on my 'to do' list without the help of the Los Angeles Police Department!" I then added quickly, "But start that clock ticking, Red. Consider the request formally made."

"I wish I could do more, me boy, but…"

"*I know,*" I interrupted disgustedly. "Red tape!"

12

THE TRAIL LEADS TO A
TALENT AGENCY

If one thing could be said about being a private detective is that it exposes you to all walks of life: The rich and the poor; the innocent and the guilty; the bright and the not so bright; the upright citizen and the dregs of society. I've run across them all in this business, and quite truthfully I can't think of a one that I would want to invite to my funeral.

Since I wasn't able to get an appointment with Taylor until after one, and definitely not about to cool my heels that morning wasting valuable time, I decided to pay a visit to Geary's agent. I used Red's phone again to call the number I'd copied down in my notebook, and ended up talking to his appointment secretary, a rather caustic individual with the phone manners of an annoying cockatoo. I was able to make an appointment to see him around ten.

The talent agency was on Sunset Boulevard. It was located on the ground floor of a two-story, Spanish style commercial building that was set back slightly from the road and landscaped with a small garden of miniature palms, some colorful bird of paradise plants, and several assorted ferns. A placard near the front door announced the 'Steinbeck Talent Agency.' The thick wooden door was unlocked, so I walked in.

"Do you have an appointment?" It was the same vitriolic woman I'd spoken to on the telephone. She had peroxide bleached blond hair and a ton of make-up, which made it difficult to place her exact age, although it was quite evident that she was well past her prime. The dress she was wearing matched her looks; cheap and immodest. The V-neck line cut lower than was socially acceptable, which made me wonder exactly what kind of talent this agency was promoting.

I told her who I was.

"The name is Logan. I have an appointment for ten."

"Lucky you," she mumbled from the corner of her mouth as she clicked the button on her intercom and spoke into it. "A Mr. Logan to see you."

A garbled reply was transmitted through the speaker of the small unit, which she translated as saying that the owner would see me shortly.

"You can take a seat in the waiting area." She waved in the general direction. The gesture carried with it an air of indifference normally reserved for blue bloods. However, I suspected this woman's was anemic.

As I walked away I heard her comment to herself something to the effect that she hated it when appointments arrived early. I looked at my watch; it was just three minutes to ten.

The adjacent waiting room was small and not particularly inviting. A handful of people were sitting about on worn leather couches, thumbing through back issues of magazines and generally looking bored. There hung on the walls a number of clients' photographs, although there were one or two of the more recognizable stars that I suspected had less to do with the agency and more to do with creating a false impression.

After about ten minutes the inner door opened and a shapely blonde walked out, pausing momentarily by the door as she self-consciously smoothed some wrinkles from her overly tight skirt. She didn't look to the right or left, but with head erect wiggled seductively out the door.

"You can go in now," announced the secretary to me, but not before giving a once over of the retreating blonde. By the disdainful expression on her face I could tell 'Miss Sunshine' didn't approve of the lady.

The owner, a Mr. Eddie Steinbeck, was sitting behind his desk as I entered the office. It was just as uncomfortable as the waiting area, and exceedingly warm. More client pictures lined two of the walls, and the third located to the rear of him had a shelf lined with numerous books. Many were on acting and acting techniques, some on speech, a couple of them dealt with pantomime, some on movement, and there was also an assortment of plays and movie scripts. Looking at the man, I wondered if he had really read all of these, or like most of his photographs just had them lying around to impress his clients.

He indicated a chair and I sat.

"What can I do for you, Mr. Logan?" he asked in a deep, melodious voice. If I had spoken to him on the phone, my visual perception of him would have been much different. He may have sounded like a leading man, but in person he was anything but. He was short and stout, with a round impish face. His dark hair was thin, greased, and combed back, and he sported a mustache which sat like a dead caterpillar between a nose that was much too large and a mouth that was exceedingly thin. Two coal black eyes stared at me in expectation of his inquiry.

"I have some questions regarding one of your clients." His bushy brows worked up and down in a nervous twitch as I answered him, and there was a slight trembling of his hands.

Recovering alcoholic I guessed. It could also explain the excessive circles and bags beneath his eyes.

"It depends what you want," he replied plainly. "If it's personal… I make it a policy to keep all that information confidential."

He reached in a box and removed a cigarette. As if it weren't stuffy enough, he lit it up and blew a smoke ring that floated like a halo above his head.

"I don't think you understand." I handed him my card. "This is about the woman murdered at the Champion studios last week… I believe she was your client."

He looked at the card after placing the cigarette between his teeth. They were desperately in need of dental work, jagged and discolored.

"Oh, yes," he replied finally comprehending. "Our dear Miss Geary… I was so sorry to hear about it." He removed the cigarette from his lips, but not before taking another drag. It was a cheap brand and the odor advertised it. "She was working on that Clemmons film…" he continued. " 'Keys to Adventure,' I recall."

"That's correct." I tried not to be obvious, but the smoke was choking me. I picked up a paper pretending to fan myself; however it was the cloud of obnoxious fumes that I was trying to whisk away. After a pause, I asked, "Had she been a client for long?"

"About ten months."

"Was she a good actress?"

"Quite confidentially," he said, leaning forward and lowering his voice in a conspiratorial manner, "she stunk. Not that I would tell the studios that, but she was really green." He sucked in more smoke and blew it out. "She couldn't act her way out of a paper bag if her life depended upon it!"

"But she did get work," I stated, surprised at his response.

"She's gotten a lot of film work lately. I'd say…." he thought for a second, "perhaps in the last six months. But before that I couldn't sell her if she was the only virgin at a sacrifice."

"That bad?" I had to laugh.

"I was getting ready to cut her loose."

"What brought about the change?"

"I don't know; and as long as I was getting my cut, I really didn't care."

"What kind of work was she getting?"

"Bit parts…minor roles." He then added as an aside, "The only type of work she could handle quite frankly. She was no Ethel Barrymore." He had replaced the cigarette into the corner of his mouth, and as he spoke an ash dropped down onto his lap. He brushed at it quickly.

"And was there any specific studio that she worked at?"

"Most of her jobs came out of Champion Studios. However, she did get the occasional assignment at some of the bigger ones…" He ticked them off on his fingers. "Selznick, Warner, RKO…"

"Was she requested by any particular person at these studios?"

"As a matter of fact, yes," he said, pausing to take another puff from his cigarette. "There was one particular person at Champion, and I wouldn't be surprised if he didn't use his influence to get her jobs at the other studios as well."

"Who? Was it a director?" I asked.

"I really can't say," he said, flicking an ash into an empty coffee cup that had suddenly materialized on his desk. "On personnel matters I usually leave all the paperwork and details to my secretary. I'd ask her. I'm more the money man… and of course I do the interviewing."

"I saw one of your interviewees leaving the office just now."

He shifted uneasily in his chair and cleared his throat. "It's my opinion regarding that person who hired her at Champion," he began, obviously anxious to change the subject, "I believe that he might have been influenced…if you get my drift…by another character."

"Who for instance?" I asked.

"Well, again it is only my opinion, but quite early on she used to come to the office with this mobster character…" He started coughing, one of those deep 'smoker's cough'. After it passed he continued, "Really shady looking guy. He would be a natural for casting in one of those gangster pictures."

"But what exactly did he look like?"

"Nothing special… a weasel." He took another long drag and started coughing again, this time for at least half a minute. It was a torture to watch him. "Again…" he finally continued, "I'd check with my secretary. He usually hung out in the waiting room whenever the girl and I had business in my office. She could probably give you a better description."

I thanked him for his time and started to leave. I paused by the door, however, and turned to ask a couple of questions that had suddenly come to mind. "Did you know her roommate, Williams— Betty Jean Williams?"

"The other girl murdered?" he asked, and I nodded. He shook his head, replying, "I can't say that I did. I don't deal with 'extras,' just models and actors. Strange coincidence, though. I read about it in the paper."

I didn't look on it as chance, but of course I wasn't going to waste my time explaining that to him. Instead I asked, "How about a Miss Hyland? Ever heard of her?"

"Nope. Any relation to the dairy?"

I also let that slide and instead thought of a third and final question. "Do you have any thoughts on who would want Miss Geary dead?"

"Only the critics," he replied with a thin smile. I guess he thought it was funny. I had trouble seeing the humor.

'Miss Sunshine' was still making an effort to look busy when I approached her at the front desk. She wasn't really fooling anyone. I spotted the nail file and bottle of varnish she was trying to hide on her lap.

"Do you mind if I ask you a few questions?" I tried flashing one of my usually disarming smiles. It turned to stone at Medusa's stare.

After several minutes of enduring the "dumb question, can't you see I'm busy" look, and inhaling her cheap overpowering perfume, I repeated my question, adding that I was a detective investigating the murder of one of their clients. The topic of death seemed to brighten her up a bit, to the extent of breaking the ice, as she finally responded, "What do you need to know?"

"I'm interested in some information about a Miss Geary; apparently she used to have a companion who would accompany her to this office. He used to wait for her in the waiting room. Could you describe him?"

"Oh, that greasy little gangster?" she replied with tact, or lack thereof. "Sure. He was a creep. But he hasn't been around for a long time…maybe six months. Rumor has it he's locked up somewhere… or pushing up lilies."

I could tell she really liked the guy. However the answer wasn't exactly what I'd asked for, so I suggested, "Could you be a little less opinionated and more objective in your description?"

I don't think she cared for my bluntness…or maybe she just didn't understand the big words, but in any case she did eventually give me what I was looking for.

"Under five foot…thin…wiry. Dark complexion… black hair, dark brown eyes…thin moustache, probably penciled. Lots of hair, most of it greased… and… oh yes, a gold tooth…" she pointed to her own right canine, "here at the front of his mouth. I saw it when he gave me one of his slimy smiles."

That description was worthy of a 'most wanted' poster, but I still had to ask, "And you believe he was associated with organized crime?"

"I can smell them a mile away." I think she was starting to relish the conversation. "This guy was really playing the part. His appearance, attitude… he even carried 'heat'. I saw it under his jacket once or twice."

"What about dress… anything particular?"

"Well," she said thoughtfully. "Nothing particular…suit, tie, overcoat, hat, and lots of flashy jewelry… although I think most of it was fake."

"Did you ever see her with anyone else besides this guy?"

"No, not that I recall," she replied vaguely. "Although I think she did come in with a younger girl once, maybe a friend, but that was pretty much it."

"Your boss said that she received most of her job opportunities from a certain individual at Champion Studios. He told me that you might know his name?"

"Sure. That's easy. Nice looking, a really handsome guy." She said this with a faraway look that I found frightening. She then added, "I wish he would request my services sometime!"

I wanted to say, 'only if he was dumb, deaf, and blind,' but I thought better of it. Perhaps I was just being unkind, but at this point I was getting impatient. When she finally came around to answering, she said the name with such reverence that I could almost hear a choir of angels accompanying it. It was Don Taylor.

I guess by my reaction she instantly realized that she might have given me something useful, because the minute she uttered his name a scowl crossed her face. It's always a pleasure when you actually learn something useful during a questioning, and with this particular witness it encouraged me to know that I could still actually squeeze blood from a turnip!

As I started to leave, I asked her, "Not much of a mosquito problem around here is there?"

"No, why?" she asked innocently.

"No particular reason," I replied as I exited the door. "I just wanted to compliment you on your choice of perfume!" I guess that was also kind of mean, but I really can't stand nasty people.

13

INVESTIGATING THE MISSING PERSON

Motion picture people are a different lot. They live in their own little celluloid world. While the rest of society has to live by one set of laws and morals, Hollywood usually makes up its own. In their court of justice, studio bosses supersede the law of the land, acting as judge and executioner to those whose soul is held as a contract in their hands.

HOLLYWOODLAND, spelled out in large white letters 30 ft. wide and 50 ft. tall, stood out on the hillside above me as I once again made my way to the Champion Studios. Erected in 1923 as a billboard promoting an upscale real estate development, it now functioned as a giant beacon symbolizing instant fame for whatever gullible moth was naïve enough to fly into its flame.

My appointment to talk to Taylor was for 1:00 p.m., and it was almost that now, but I decided first to take a trip over to the Make-up and Hairstyling Department, which was located in a two-story white stucco build-ing toward the center of the lot. I was curious if Miss Wilson had heard anything from Fran Adams, and figured that it might also give me an excuse to snoop around her workspace while I was at it.

Connie Wilson was in her mid-twenties, with trans-lucent skin, large black eyes and dark brown hair styled in a "buster brown" cut. She was of medium build and wearing a smock similar to the one I had seen Adams dressed in during my first visit to the studio.

"Any word from Miss Adams?" I asked the minute I entered the room.

"Nothing yet… Mister? I'm sorry I forgot your name," she replied as I flashed my I.D.

"Logan, Tom Logan." I looked around the room. It was divided into several smaller working areas. "Does she have a space here?"

She said yes and showed me over to a partitioned area complete with salon chair, lighted mirror, and counter covered with enough brushes and combs to satisfy the grooming habits of a small nation. I started searching through some of her belongings under the uncertain eyes of my impromptu guide. While sift-ing through these articles I asked her a number of questions related to Adams' mood, or any comments she had made when last she had seen her.

"She seemed nervous and distracted," Wilson admitted thoughtfully. "But then she has been since…" She stopped suddenly and bit her lip.

I looked up quickly and asked, "Since what?" She replied quietly, "Since she got into trouble."

I thought about this a minute and asked as tactfully as possible if she could further explain. She blushed slightly, and then continued, "She's been in this condition for at least two, maybe three months. I think she's undecided what to do when she starts showing. She's already wearing loose clothes."

"Did she ever indicate who the father was?"

"No, she's never let on."

"Any guesses?"

"I wouldn't know," she answered curtly.

I decided to change the subject.

"You told me over the phone that she didn't give any indication on Friday that she wouldn't be in?

"That's correct. In fact, I remember her saying as she left that she would see me on Monday."

I got down on the floor and searched underneath Adams' work bench and then ran my hands along the open spaces between the counter and the wall. I also ran my fingers around the edges of her mirror. I wasn't exactly sure what I was looking for, but whatever it was, I'm sure Connie Wilson could see that I was determined to find it. I left digging through Adams' trash can for last. Luckily it wasn't too full; however, I did find something of interest: a crumbled piece of paper torn from her calendar. It had Friday's date and the words 'Get Key C'. I showed it to Wilson.

"Is that Adams' handwriting?" I asked.

"Yes, that looks like Fran's," she replied, observing it keenly.

"Any idea what it's referring to?"

"No, I'm afraid not."

I took the scrap of paper from her, inserted it safely between the pages of my notebook, and then slipped it back into my inside jacket pocket.

"Would it be possible to get Adams' address and phone number?"

"Sure, I can give it to you." She started to reach for a pencil and pad, but paused to ask:

"You don't think she's in any sort of trouble do you?"

"To be honest," I replied, "I really can't say."

She wasn't pleased with the answer, but at that moment it was the only one I could provide. Accepting my poor attempt at consolation, she jotted down the information and handed it to me. Taking it, I exchanged it for my card.

"If you happen to hear anything further, I can be reached at this number," I instructed, and thanked her for her time.

I thought about the words written on the scrap of paper as I left the building. They were a reminder of some sort, that much was clear. But what 'Key C' was, or whether it held any significance to her disappearance was a mystery yet to be solved. I was still mulling this over in my mind when I almost ran into one of the custodians carrying some trash to a container. That reminded me of something else I had been curious about and decided to make one more detour before contacting Taylor.

"When do they pick up trash around here?" I asked startling him.

"Every Wednesday," he replied, "though we usually incinerate the paper trash ourselves."

I thanked him and headed over in the direction of the European set. I decided to retrace Fran Adams' movements based on Mr. Smith's description. These first led away from, and then back to, the crime scene. I particularly searched out any areas, most notably trash containers near the sound stages, where she could safely dispose of an item without fear of being seen. Fortune was with me, and after digging through several bins, I stumbled upon an oily rag that was wrapped around some broken pieces of pottery. I assembled them and they formed a cup.

Wrapping them up again, I tucked them neatly into my outer jacket pocket. It seems now I'd some physical evidence to corroborate Smith's story.

I finally made it to the Production Office about thirty-five minutes late. I was told by Lana, who turned out to be a small mousey girl, that an impromptu screening of the "rushes" from Friday's shooting had been called by the director.

"The camera crew and the production staff are over at Grauman's Chinese Theatre now watching the 'out-takes,'" she informed me. "Mr. Taylor, however, has left word that a driver was to take you over when you arrive." She picked up her phone and immediately contacted Transportation.

It was only a few minutes' drive to Grauman's theatre, an opulent building adorned in full Oriental splendor. Two large red columns crowned by fierce iron masks flanked both sides of the entrance supporting a traditional slanted bronze roof. A 30 ft. dragon carved in white stone was mounted on the wall above the main doors, while two giant stone Heaven Dogs stood vigilant on each side guarding the entrance. It was built a little less than three years ago at a price of $2,000,000 and was opened to the public in a ceremony that for spectacle can never be matched. Cecil B. DeMille's "The King of Kings" premiered that night and thousands of people flooded Hollywood Boulevard to near riot proportions, undoubtedly hoping to catch a glimpse of their favorite star as they paraded in.

The driver stopped opposite the entrance. As he came around to open my door I asked if he could wait.

"I'd like to return to the studio after I finish talking to Mr. Taylor," I explained. I still had it in mind to visit the Transportation Department before wrapping it up that day.

He brought his hand up to his cap in a semblance of a salute and mumbled smartly, "Very good, sir. If I can't find a place to park, I'll circle the block. Just wait by the entrance when you're ready to return."

I thanked him and stepped out onto the busy sidewalk. I noticed at my appearance a few people turning and others straining their necks to get a better look. I guess they were expecting to see somebody of importance. Being this was Hollywood, no doubt they were hoping that it might even be a star! I actually started to feel self-important, that is until I caught their expressions of disappointment as they turned away. There was one individual, however, who kept his interest; a man I unfortunately half noticed being less cautious than normal that afternoon. Maybe it was just because I was feeling the effects of a long day or simply distracted, but as I passed into the lobby I hardly observed the keen eyes watching me from the shadows of the forecourt near the tall lotus-shaped fountain.

As soon as I walked into the foyer I was immediately approached by a young employee who told me that the theatre was closed for a special party, adding that it would reopen for the evening performance. I flashed my card and told him that I had business inside.

He escorted me through the elegant Oriental themed lobby decorated with large murals depicting life in an ancient Chinese village. Thick red carpet interlaced with patterns of gold flowers stretched out before our feet, as we crossed between tall ruby colored pillars that reached up to a ceiling ornately decorated and painted gold. The entire lobby was illuminated by chandeliers designed as Chinese lanterns, their bulbs casting a warm, almost subtle glow. As we proceeded toward the auditorium we passed heavily curtained alcoves filled with silk screens, various pieces of Chinese artifacts and traditional black lacquered tables and chairs. Eventually we reached an antiquely decorated golden door that led into the auditorium.

It was dark when we stepped inside and a film was being projected up on the massive screen. My eyes took some time in getting adjusted, but when they did I was able to make out a small group of men sitting in the center section, the large numbers of surrounding empty seats making them look small and insignificant.

The scene being shown in the movie up on the screen looked familiar. It was the battle segment that had been shot on Friday. It was obviously a rough cut, for the sequences were noticeably out of order and certain elements were missing. A clapper was also displayed for both the start and ending of the clip to identify the segments.

A combination of cigar and cigarette smoke could be seen drifting past the broad shaft of light cast from the projector, puffs of vapor rising up like signals from an Indian village just prior to an attack. As the final clip on the screen faded to black I heard a familiar voice yell, "Can we turn up the lights?" It was Clemmons giving an instruction to the projection room.

I walked down the richly carpeted aisle as the auditorium gradually became illuminated by a single enormous chandelier adorned with an elaborate sunburst base. It was located directly above me in the center of the ceiling. Next, I watched as two large, heavy red curtains, embroidered with images of golden palms, slid smoothly shut, completely concealing the screen.

"Logan!" Taylor had spotted me and was calling from his seat. He got up and made his way along the row. "I can spare you a few minutes," he said in reaching me, "but not much more. We only have the theatre for another hour."

"Don't you have facilities at the studio for viewing films?"

"We have a theatre, but unfortunately it was booked for another production. A continuity question came up in our meeting on Saturday and we didn't want to delay shooting any longer than we had to." He dropped into one of the comfortable, plush red velvet seats near the end of the aisle and I did likewise. "Now," he began once we got settled. "I can add little to what you already know. I was on the opposite side of the set when the murder occurred. Next to the director." He waved a hand in the general direction of his associates. "Any one of them could vouch for me. I wasn't aware that anything was wrong until after the girl was murdered."

"Did you know her well?" I asked, taking command of the interview.

"Not well," he said, pausing to take a drag from his cigarette.

"That's not what I heard from her agency. They claim that you've requested her for numerous jobs."

"If you're asking if I knew her personally; then my answer still stands," he replied coolly. "However, professionally is another story. Like some of the other struggling actors out there, I felt sorry for the kid and decided to give her a leg up."

"So you've helped other struggling actors?"

"Why not? These are tough times. I'm lucky to have a job, so why not help others if I have a chance."

"Like for instance?"

"I can't name them off the top of my head, but you can ask my production secretary if you're interested."

"Had Geary been on the picture for long?"

"She only came on board a few days ago." He took another drag at his cigarette.

"Was she liked?"

"I believe so."

"Do you think she had any enemies?"

"I really couldn't say." He suddenly became impatient. "Listen, Logan, hasn't it occurred to you that you might be looking in the wrong direction? I sent Mattie over to you because I believe someone within the studio was threatening her life. It seems to me that whoever that person was decided to strike, but hit the wrong target."

"Like for instance that guy hanging around the set? The one you referred to as a mobster?"

"It's possible."

"Miss Hyland said you suggested me for the case. Why?"

He smiled, but it looked forced. "I thought that would be obvious. You helped me out of a jam… She was in trouble…I figured you were the right person for the case." He paused, and then added as an afterthought, "Perhaps I was mistaken."

I ignored the last jab, and proceeded rapidly to another question.

"So from your previous statements it seems that Miss Hyland felt comfortable enough to confide in you?"

"Yes, we're friends. Why not?"

I waited to see if he would add more and when he didn't I asked, "So, if this 'mobster' has indeed sent this warning, what could he be warning her to keep quiet about?"

"I was hoping you could answer that," he responded tersely. "However, if I were you I'd be spending more time trying to discover an answer to that question and less chasing air with these queries about Geary!"

Clemmons called over indicating that Taylor was needed again, so I fired off one last question which seemed to catch him by surprise.

"Were you aware that Fran Adams hasn't reported into work today?"

He took another puff at his cigarette.

"No. I was not."

I noticed his hand shaking slightly.

"Any ideas why?"

"I'm afraid not."

He tried to give the impression of not caring, but I could tell that the information had made him as skittish as a long- tailed cat in a room full of rocking chairs.

Having completed the interview I left the theatre and stepped out into the courtyard. The day was bright, and for a moment I was blinded by the sun. I took a few steps forward when I felt a hand grip my shoulder from behind and turn me violently. As we faced each other he hissed, "You're not trying to double cross me, are you?"

14

AN UNEXPECTED ENCOUNTER

I need... I need...I need. That was all I was
hearing from this guy. So do people in hell
need ice water... and what does he expect me
to do about that? Perhaps it was my fault
for stringing him along. You don't dangle a
sausage in front of a dog and not expect him
to keep nipping at it.

The instant I felt his hand on my shoulder I tensed, preparing myself both physically and mentally for an attack. Instantly I started calculating distances and possible points of weaknesses that could work to my advantage. This, of course, depended upon the scenario ...a club... a gun... a knife. However, the moment I recognized my assailant as

Smith, and that he held no other weapon than the two-edged one that came out of his mouth, I relaxed.

"You're not double crossing me, are you?" he repeated, only this time with emphasis. I figure he thought I hadn't heard him the first time.

"I don't have the slightest idea what you're talking about," I responded, firmly removing his hand from my shoulder. Surprisingly he reached with his other into my jacket pocket and removed its contents: the oily rag with the pieces of broken cup.

He started to say something about selling him out, but cut it short, as glancing down at the object in his hand, he expressed first surprise and then embarrassment at what he held. I guess he was under the impression that I had the book on my person. An awkward pause followed in which he readily recovered asking, "Do we have a deal or what?" He replaced the objects back into my pocket. "Did you convince the police to back off?"

"I've talked to them. I think they believe your story."

"And what about my book?"

"I told you I need time." I said it between clenched teeth. Quite honestly, I was getting tired of his persistence.

"Well, I think you're stalling," he snapped back. "I don't think you have it at all." When I didn't respond, he eyed me keenly. "The police have it, don't they?"

I avoided answering again, but replied instead, "I don't appreciate you following me."

He looked slyly at me for a moment and then responded, "They do have it!"

Just then my driver pulled up, and noticing this, Smith decided to make a hasty exit, but not before calling over his shoulder, "In that case, Logan, we have no further business!"

The chauffeur drove me directly to the Transportation Department located on one corner of the studio lot. It consisted of two smaller buildings that housed the offices, a large garage, and four gasoline pumps beneath a tall roof supported by four sturdy metal beams. A medium-sized paved lot was located at the center of the surrounding buildings. Here various studio trucks, generators, movie cars, and crew transportation vehicles sat parked in numbered spaces.

I checked in with Terry Muller, Head of Transportation, a small, balding man with a prominent belly and a bushy nicotine stained moustache. I questioned him with the view of learning something about their operation.

"Do you have a log book?" I asked looking around.

"Sure," he said, retrieving a ledger sized, bounded book and pushing it across the counter.

I leafed through it, and after observing several pages, came to the realization that the log was rarely used. The last entries were a month back and even those were sporadic. I commented about that and he responded, "They're kind of lax when it comes to following rules around here." He seemed embarrassed. "I brought it up to the studio heads, but they sort of brushed it off. I guess they have more important things to worry about."

"What about the keys?" I asked, and he pointed to a mounted glass cabinet with a lock just to the right of the door. There were several rows of pegs inside, some of which had keys dangling from them, and each with a tag and a number attached. "Do you keep that locked?"

Again he looked embarrassed as he answered, "The lock's broken and I haven't been able to find a replacement."

"Then these keys can be removed at any hour, night or day, without the knowledge of the staff, and the vehicles taken for personal use, if need be?"

"I'm afraid that's the long and short of it." He then added quickly, "However, they do need a key to the office when we're away."

"And who would have access to that?"

His countenance dimmed as he replied, "Janitors, staff, drivers…"

"In other words," I interrupted, "just about anyone."

He nodded.

'So, scratch that avenue of investigation,' I thought to myself as I moved out into the sunlight. I'd hit a dead end. As studio security goes this one had more holes in it than a colander. First, Smith was able to bypass the gate with help from the inside and now I discovered that anyone could obtain the use of a vehicle without leaving a paper trail. 'I guess you can't bat 1000 every time you're up at the plate,' I consoled myself, shrugging my broad shoulders.

After finishing my business at the studio I returned to my office. As I stepped off the elevator I could hear the sharp peal of my telephone echoing down the hall. I struggled several minutes in an effort to unlock the door, cussing Smith throughout the ordeal; for ever since he had broken into my office that night I had been having trouble with the lock. All the while I could hear the persistent ringing inside and I grew ever more frustrated with each failed attempt. It was close, but eventually I was able to get the door open and catch the phone on its last ring. I lifted the receiver just in time to hear Red's greeting.

"I got a piece of interesting information, me boy," he said with evident excitement. "We got our motive for da murder." He didn't wait for me to answer, but continued, "Blackmail!"

"So, I take it Father McCarthy came through?"

"In clover!" he responded. "Dates, payoffs, references to various pieces of evidence…"

"And names?" I asked anxiously. Here his enthusiasm waned.

"Dat, Mary is still working on. Sadly, it turns out dat da pictograms refer to da people involved and even those seem to be further disguised."

"What's her thoughts? Does she feel she could work them out?"

"I keep asking her, and always her answer is da same, 'Once I find da key!' He then added with frustration, "It's enough to drive a man to drink!"

"That wouldn't take much."

"How'd you make out at da studio?"

"Adams is still missing, but I found something that may or may not offer a clue to her whereabouts."

"What's dat?"

"A reminder she'd left on a page of her calendar. I found it in her trash."

"Do you think it might give you a lead on Adams?" Red asked hopefully.

"Perhaps, if I can figure out what 'Key C' is," I replied. "I also did some digging around the garbage containers near the set and discovered a broken cup, which could be the one Adams disposed of. It was wrapped in an oily rag, so it seems like someone was trying to hide it."

"Then Smith's tale may not be blarney, as we would say in da ole country."

"Well, let's say it's a possibility," I replied cautiously. "And speaking of Smith, I also made contact with him, or should I say that he made contact with me…"

"What did dat rascal want?" Red interrupted. "As if I couldn't guess."

"The book, what else… I think he was disappointed with my answer."

Red chuckled on the other end and when he'd fin-ished, I continued, "I finally got around to interviewing Taylor, but quite honestly he's a hard nut to crack. After I left you, I decided to visit Geary's agent and found out that it was Taylor who had cast her for the role of the nurse. In fact, he had been actively getting her work at Champion and other studios for the past six months. When I confronted him about this he gave me an answer that on the surface seems reasonable, but I'm not sure if I'm totally buying it. He's a difficult one to figure out."

"Still waters run deep, me boy!"

"Yeah. Well this guy's the Mariana Trench!" I then concluded: "And finally I checked on the car with Transportation. I found their bookkeeping impossible."

"So there's no hope of tracing da automobile ei-ther to Smith or his doppelganger, yer telling me?"

"I'm afraid not. The security at that studio is a nightmare."

A long pause followed, and then Red asked, "Were you able to talk to any of Adams' co-workers?"

I started to answer when an idea suddenly struck me. "By chance, was a pregnancy mentioned anywhere in the book?"

"I believe it was," he said thoughtfully. "Why, do you have an idea?"

"I might. Tell her to use 'Fran Adams' for the pic-togram linked to the pregnancy. It could be *her* key."

For all intents and purposes, Fran Adams had become my number one suspect, or at the least a definite person of interest. The only problem was she was nowhere to be found. After calling the studio the next morning to verify that she still hadn't reported, I decided to make it my priority to see if I could trace her.

The Santa Ana winds had blown in from the desert early that morning, making my walk up Melrose Avenue hot and uncomfortable. I'd tried calling her residence after talking to the studio, but received no answer. I therefore decided to check out her place first hand.

Her residence was located a few blocks from both the Paramount and RKO studios. RKO, incidentally, had recently received a lot of notoriety from its release of "Hell's Angels." An enormous poster with the tag line: "Thrilling Multi-Million Dollar Air Spectacle—directed by Howard Hughes" caught my eye as I walked by the studio complex.

I located her house at the address that was given to me. It was in the Craftsman style and buried amongst a number of similar looking homes located on that block. It seemed dark and deserted as I walked up, but I decided to knock on the door anyway.

Not surprisingly there came no answer. I made a quick examination along both sides of the building and then walked around to the back. It was shut up tighter than Noah's ark. I returned to the front yard and started to examine the contents of her mailbox when I was hailed by a middle-aged woman dressed in a house dress and slippers.

"She's not home," the woman explained coming toward me, and I couldn't help but notice that it was said with a hint of suspicion. "Can I help you?"

I handed her my card and asked, "Do you have any idea where she might be?"

"Why?" she asked, reading what I had given her. "Is she in any sort of trouble?"

"She hasn't reported to work in a couple days…"

"And so they send a detective for that?"

"No, " I laughed. "There's been some trouble at the studio, and they were concerned about her safety."

"Oh yes. I read about it in the paper." She became more animated. "Some actress got murdered. They never said how she was killed however?"

"Have you seen Miss Adams recently?" I asked, purposely ignoring her question.

Both Red and I were playing this pretty close to the chest and we didn't want to release too many details during the course of the investigation. I was surprised that he'd given out that information about Smith to the press, but then again Smith was our chief suspect at the time, and getting his description out to the public would seem the surest way of tracking him. Of course that had all changed now.

She paused a moment, perhaps put off by my sudden shift in discussion, and then answered, "I saw her late Friday…" She suddenly reached out her hand. "I'm her neighbor by the way. Linda Miller." I shook it and then she continued, "It looked like she was planning to be away for some time. I saw her loading a couple of suitcases into her car."

"Did you speak with her?"

She shook her head.

"I was entertaining a gentleman at the time. I'd just happened to look out the side window and see her."

"Was anyone with her?"

"No. She was alone."

"What kind of car was it?"

"A red-colored, four-door, Pontiac sedan."

"Did you notice anything strange at all?"

She shook her head again. "No. Nothing. I just figured she might be taking a vacation or going to visit her parents."

"Do you know where they live?"

"No." She thought for a second and then added, "But perhaps her boyfriend could tell you."

"Where can I find him?"

"He's a writer at the Chaplin Studios." She started snapping her fingers in a pointless gesture of trying to jog her memory. "I think his name is Steve…I'm not sure what his last name is, however."

Leaving Adams' neighborhood I started to feel hungry and consulted my watch. Discovering it was noon,

I searched out the local business district and stumbled upon a food automat. I decided to keep it simple, just a sandwich and some coffee, but digging into my pockets realized that I needed some change first. I cashed in my dollar for some nickels at the centrally placed cashier, somewhat bored young woman, who had her face buried in a romance pulp, where I could find a public phone. She pointed a thumb over her shoulder, never losing a beat as she turned a page and gnawed furiously on her gum.

I entered one of two phone booths and dialed the Operator. She connected me to Central Dispatch, which was located at City Hall and they in turn rang up the Homicide Division. As I waited for Red to pick up, I glanced over at a pile of newspapers which were sitting on a counter opposite the booth. The headlines read: SHANTY TOWNS NOW CALLED "HOOVERVILLES" IN U.S.

I remembered thinking that the country had really hit rock bottom. The economic depression was not only being felt in the U.S., but economists were predicting that it could eventually spread across the globe as well. It began with the stock market crash in October of the previous year, 'Black Tuesday' they were now calling it. President Hoover was trying to reverse the down turn by proposing various volunteer efforts, and just this last June Congress passed the Smoot-Hawley Tariff Act. Would any of this work? Who knows? But I was confident in time we would pull through. America had gone through a lot worse in its history and it had always seemed to bounce back.

"Thomas?" purred the familiar Irish brogue.

"Yes. I was just checking in," I replied. "Anything new?"

"As a matter of fact…"

15

QUESTIONS AND ANSWERS

*Making inquiries is like eating an artichoke;
each leaf representing a question. Every time
you expose a truth one is peeled away only
to discover another. In the beginning it is
frustrating and seemingly impossible, but if you
keep working long enough at it you'll eventually
reach its' heart and redeem your reward.*

I put my coins in a slot and removed my selection
by lifting the narrow glass door and slipping the
plate through the slit. It was a rather bland ham
and cheese on dry white bread, which I washed down
quickly with strong black coffee. As I helped myself to
a second cup I reviewed the conversation I'd just had
with Red over the telephone. First off he told me that
Ballistics had connected the gun that Soames had giv-
en us with the bullet dug out of Geary's body.

"Estimated 158 grain … consistent with a .38 caliber bullet," he read, summarizing the findings. I could hear him shuffle the papers. "Autopsy reports describe a single gunshot wound to da back of da head… with no charring of da wound and no residue in da wound track…"

"And no new surprises," I added dryly, cutting him off. "What about prints?"

"They couldn't find any," he continued. "It's just as we suspected, either da killer used gloves or da weapon was wiped clean after it was fired."

"If you ask me I'd say that it was most probably the latter," I suggested, remembering a number of rags sitting on the bench at the set. "How are you doing with the lawyers?"

"Talk about da 'luck of da Irish,' they said dat they should have an 'injunction' ready by tomorrow morning." He then added matter-of-factly, "Of course it might've had something to do with me calling da mayor."

"That could explain it," I commented dryly. "That's the fastest I've ever seen the legal department act." I then requested, "Mind if I tag along with you tomorrow when you check out the bank?"

"Ya took the words right out of me mouth."

"I'm curious to see those records…" I began.

"But it gets even better," Red interrupted. "It seems she has a safe deposit box."

"Does the injunction allow us access to those materials as well?"

"I'm looking for a locksmith now."

"How did Mary make out with my suggestion?"

"More good news, but I'll let her tell ya herself!"

Red put Kelly on the line.

"I tried what you asked me," she began, "and it worked. It was the key I was looking for. It turns out that the pictograms were a cipher, which translated indicates a book, chapter, and verse from the Bible. In this case I took the section related to the pregnancy, applied the name and worked backwards. Based on that, the pictogram heading to that section now reads; Genesis 2:20. In case you don't have a Bible handy, this verse mentions the first man by name and thus connects it to Fran Adams."

"I won't pretend to understand entirely what you're talking about," I replied laughing, "but will it work on the others?"

"I believe so, though I won't kid you, I'm struggling with them at the moment. I believe the same method should apply, but it's proving more difficult because the names themselves are not as simple." She then concluded, "A combination of verses might be the answer."

Red came back on the line and asked what progress I'd made on my end. I related the details of my conversation with Adams' neighbor, ending the narration with the request, "I think you should put an A.P.B. out on Adams. From what I've learned so far, it looks like she's on the run. I feel it's more important than ever now to pull her in. If she's not guilty of the murder, we do know that she's somehow involved. Quite frankly, it's my impression that she probably knows something."

"You think she's running scared?" Red asked.

"I think she might be in danger. She could possibly be able to finger the killer."

"I'll get da A.P.B. out da moment I hang up with ya," Red replied with urgency. "So, what's yar next move?"

"Stop by the Chaplin Studios, and hopefully locate this writer boyfriend of hers. I'm hoping he might give us a lead to her whereabouts.

The Chaplin Studios was located on the corner of Sunset and LaBrea. It was built in 1917 by Charlie Chaplin in the style of an old English village. The architect took the surrounding clapboard houses and placed a Tudor mansion facade complete with brick walls and chimneys. I walked through a small, beautifully landscaped garden of brightly colored flowers and neatly trimmed grass located at the entrance of the administration building, and stepped through the gray ornate front door which led into Reception. From here I was directed to the Production Office where I waited for some time sitting upon a comfortable couch.

I was told by the silver-haired receptionist that there was a Steven Miller on the writing staff and he, as well as the other writers, was presently in conference with Mr. Chaplin. She also added that he should be available shortly. A tea cart came up while I was waiting and an extremely polite young woman with a British accent asked if I wanted anything. I declined. A few minutes later another person entered the room, an attractive woman who I instantly recognized as Paulette Goddard. The actress was there for a fitting. Evidently she was co-starring in the studio's most recent production "City Lights." With much fanfare they rushed her off to Wardrobe.

Finally after cooling my heels for about half an hour, an inner office door opened and several men filed out, included Mr. Chaplin himself, a small agile man with intense dark brown eyes and a mass of curly dark brown hair, slightly graying at the temples. The receptionist I'd talked to immediately got up from her desk and intercepted a tall, blond man who soon after came over in my direction.

"I'm Steve Miller," he said offering his hand. "I was told you wanted to see me?"

I handed him my card. "It all depends. Are you acquainted with a woman called Fran Adams?"

"Yes. We use to date," he responded somewhat perplexed.

"Why?"

155

"If you've been reading the papers you're probably aware that a murder occurred at her studio." I waited and he nodded his head. "Well, we need to question her. It seems she decided to take this inopportune time to skip town, and I was wondering if you've any ideas where she might've gone off to?"

"I couldn't say. We broke off several weeks ago."

"How long had you been dating?"

"About a year. Maybe slightly longer."

"And can I ask why you broke up?"

"I'd rather not."

"I'm sorry," I apologized, "but I have to ask. It may have some bearing on the case."

"She got involved with someone at the studio."

"Any ideas who?"

"Not exactly, but I have my suspicions."

"Which are?"

"Look, what's this have to do with me?"

"I was told that you might help us?"

"How?"

"For one, to locate her parents."

"Sure, they live in Santa Barbara."

"Was she originally from there?"

"Yes. Born and raised. Her father is a successful businessman. He has a general store. Carries about everything you could imagine. Fran used to help out there when she wasn't in school."

"Good student?"

"She said she was. Although she admitted once that she was probably a better athlete. She got medals for just about every sport in high school… archery and such. He then added with a trace of pride, "Even in some of the sports that guys usually excel in."

If Geary had been shot by an arrow that bit of information would've been interesting.

"Do you have her parents' address or phone number?"

"I can't remember the address, but I have their phone number."

"Could you please call Detective Sean Clancy at Homicide Division and give him the information?" I asked, as I scribbled Red's number on a page from my notebook, tore it out, and handed it to him.

"Returning to something you said earlier. You mentioned that you had suspicions about who she may be dating? Want to share them?"

He thought for a second, and then making up his mind, replied harshly, "One of the directors on this picture she's working on!"

Red picked me up the following morning at my apartment. It would be about a thirty-minute ride to the branch where Geary had banked, located on Sunset Boulevard. During the ride Red revealed, to my excitement, that late last night Mary had finally solved the remaining pictograms.

"Dat little book has turned up more than a few surprises, Thomas," Red explained as he turned the 1928 Ford Model A Tudor Sedan onto West 3rd.

"How's that?"

"Not only was Fran Adams named, but listen to this line up: Clemmons, Soames, Taylor, and Hyland. Da blackmailer had something on them all."

"Which means we're more or less back to square one. Any one of them now has a motive to kill Geary. In other words, we've more suspects than we know what to do with."

"So it would seem, me boy," Red said, waving a car around that was following too close. "But let's analyze this a moment. Miss Williams was murdered by a male. That much we're certain of. So it would seem dat we could eliminate da list by two… da two women."

He took a right at LaBrea Avenue.

"However," I added, "there are still too many questions floating out there about Adams. What was the deal with the coffee cup? And why has she run away? As I mentioned yesterday over the telephone, she knows something. And then, what about my client? She never mentioned being blackmailed. Why did she keep that away from me? I'll need to question her further on that point."

We passed the Tar Pits on our right.

The LaBrea Tar Pits or Rancho LaBrea Tar Pits are a group of asphalt pits located within Hancock Park. For approximately 10,000 years tar had been seeping up from the ground at this location, and over the centuries animals of various kinds have fallen in and their bones preserved. These are presently being excavated in the park and the finds displayed in the L.A. Natural History Museum.

"Do ya still believe her claims about being threatened?" Red asked after a long pause during which he'd been concentrating on the traffic that was heavier than normal that morning.

"It still could be true," I conceded. "Perhaps the blackmailer was the author of the letter."

"Then do ya think dat she still might've been da original target?"

"I guess anything's possible, but quite honestly," I replied shaking my head, "I'm still having trouble with it. Call it a gut feeling, but it doesn't feel right. And for that matter, I'm also having difficulty figuring exactly where Adams fits into all this."

"And what about Smith?" Red asked, turning onto Sunset. "Is he our blackmailer? He claimed da book was his, but yet we're pretty sure he isn't the murderer... *or are we?*"

"True," I reasoned. "I'm sure he didn't kill the Williams girl, but it's only his word that he didn't kill Geary."

"And then," he added, pulling the car into a space that had opened up in front of the bank, "there are still Soames and Taylor. Neither was near da property boxes during da time of da murder, but either could've been at the Williams' apartment dat night."

"There's also the possibility that we overlooked one other point," I said thoughtfully as we exited the car. "Maybe the killer didn't need to be by the boxes at all to accomplish his or her end."

We were greeted with a measure of reserve by the manager, who seemed to be waiting in anticipation for our arrival. He intercepted us the moment we stepped in through the double doors and steered us quite smoothly away from his customers and into a small office located in the back. All the requested records were gathered for us and laid out neatly on a desk. After verifying that we were satisfied with the arrangements he excused himself, leaving us alone to delve into this veritable treasure trove.

"There's no doubt about it," Red said after we had spent some time running through the piles of transactions. "These records verify it… blackmail, clear and simple." He ran his finger down a column of figures. "There were a number of deposits made in her account over da past months. They are of a fairly sizable amount and for da most part deposited in cash." He indicated several entries. "Each deposit was made at fairly consistent intervals, usually varying by only a couple of days." He had brought the journal with him.

Removing it from his pocket he handed it to me, requesting that I compare the diary's entries with the bank receipts.

After several minutes I replied with confidence, "See for yourself." I handed him back the book. "The amounts deposited and those in the journal match up exactly; arranged in rows just like a ledger under each of the names. However, I don't know if you noticed it," I said pointing over to one of the columns, "but there is something curious here. While Hyland, Soames, Adams and Clemmons are all credited in entries over the last five to six months, Taylor does not have even one payment listed under his name."

"Perhaps," Red suggested, "he was da newest victim of da bunch?"

"That's possible," I reasoned. "It may be that the blackmailer hadn't gotten a chance to put the touch on him yet, or on the other hand it could be that Taylor just decided not to give in to the demands."

Red examined the page closer. "Ya know, Thomas, now that ya mention it, I don't see much at all about him here, aside from his name. At least some of da others have a few details written alongside their entries."

"Well, from what I could see Hyland doesn't have much written either... and the payment under her name seems to have gone back the longest. Perhaps we shouldn't draw too many conclusions until we first examine the safe deposit box. We may find more evidence there."

When we had concluded our investigation of the records, a teller escorted us into the vault. Here, under the eyes of both the manager and assistant manager, the safe deposit box was removed using a local locksmith, who pulled the lock. The procedure took an hour, after which we were again left alone to examine its contents in a private cubicle put aside for us. The items were quite revealing.

"Letters, notes, and photographs," Red listed off as he sifted through the pile he poured out onto the table. "Each one of these could be a potential disaster for da victim and heyday for da press."

I noticed some particular photos and slid them over to Red. He shook his head when he saw them and commented, "Well at least we know now what da blackmailer had on Miss Hyland!"

"And these letters suggest infidelity on Clemmons part," I continued. "And here is evidence that Soames was tied into vice… mainly alcohol and drugs…Adams was pregnant out of wedlock…but…" I thumbed through them a second time to be sure. "I still don't see anything on Taylor."

In light of this new discovery we decided that each of the suspects would now have to be presented with this evidence and reexamined. I decided that my next move was to confront my client, and although locating the missing hairdresser was still on the top of my list, I couldn't escape the fact that questioning Taylor, Soames, and Clemmons could be of equal importance.

"I know ya got a lot on yar plate, finding this hair-dresser and all. Do ya want me to send some men to question these others?"

"Did Adams' ex-boyfriend, Miller, reach you?"

"He'd called Homicide late last night, but unfortunately I'd left," he replied. "The desk took the message however. He's given us da parent's phone number."

"Have you tried calling it?"

"I did this morning before I picked you up, but I got no answer. I plan to try again later."

"Well then, I guess there's not much more I can do regarding Adams until we reach them," I concluded. "No, leave the questioning to me. Appointment or not, I'll try catching Taylor, Soames, and Clemmons at the studio this afternoon."

16

THE FACTS REGARDING BLACKMAIL

If there is one type of criminal that I cannot stomach it's a blackmailer. A revolting little creature who sits in the center of his web waiting for some convenient fat fly to come along so he could suck the blood out of him. He's that miscreant of society that I find particular pleasure in crushing under foot.

Examining Geary's records and opening her safe deposit box had confirmed what we expected, and although it set to rest one question, it opened up a myriad of others. As I stated from the beginning this case was not going to be a walk in the park.

I called the studio before leaving the bank and reached Rita in the Production Office.

"Hi, Logan," she answered with a slight tease to her voice. "Missed me?"

"Sure Doll, but this isn't a social call. Who's in today?"

"Everyone in Production. The rest of the non-essential crew is off. There's been a big blow up and production has temporarily been shut down."

"What's the beef?"

"I'm not sure, but I think these murders are starting to affect the picture."

"Are Hyland and Soames also off?"

"Yes." she replied simply. "Just the Production Staff's on site."

"Does that include Clemmons and Taylor?"

"Sure. Both are right in the middle of it. And from the sound of it, they won't be going anywhere soon."

"Thanks. I'll probably see you later."

"Can't wait," she signed off with a hint of promise.

I dialed Miss Hyland's home number and reached her just as she was going out the door.

"What's up, Logan?"

"We need to meet."

"I have an appointment for a fitting."

"Cancel it. This is important."

"I can't. It took me a month to get it." She paused, and then suggested, "What about I pick you up and you can tell me on the way?"

"What I have to say, you might not want said in public."

There was another pause, only this one was longer, and then she replied, "I'll take that chance."

I told her where she could collect me, and about twenty minutes later a limo pulled up.

"Hop in, Logan," Hyland called out as she cranked down the limo's window. The chauffeur started to make a move to open the door, but I waved him off opting to assist myself into the rear seat next to her. The minute I shut the door he pulled out into traffic.

"You always take a limo shopping?" I had to ask. I could well imagine the looks I'd get if I were to take this buggy to the Grand Central Market some weekday afternoon.

"Just when I'm feeling lazy," she replied carelessly. "Now tell me, what's all this about? Why the urgency?"

I reached into my pocket and produced the photographs; a peep show in which she played a starring role. At the sight of them she paled noticeably and quickly placed her hands across them as if to blot them out. I started to say something, but she nodded toward the driver and indicated that I should wait.

We remained silent for the rest of the journey, which culminated at the Bullocks Wilshire on Wilshire Boulevard. It was completed a year ago catering to affluent shoppers. This luxury department store was housed in an Art Deco building which included a 241-foot tower sheathed in tarnished copper. At its peak was a light that was lit at night and could be seen for miles throughout the basin.

Hyland's chauffeur pulled into the rear entrance and we were greeted promptly by a valet. A few steps and we entered its interior, 230,000 square feet of retail space. The foyer was breathtaking with its travertine floor and eggshell painted walls ornately dressed up in hand carved moldings. A concierge immediately approached us and, with military efficiency, ascertained what department we were interested in. He then escorted us, personally, to a bank of elevators the likes of which I'd never seen before. The doors were finished in gunmetal, brass, and nickel, and glistened in the bright artificial lights. We got off at one of the upper floors and entered a room named for Louis XVI. This boutique dealt with designer dresses, which obviously were on my client's shopping list. An exceedingly prim elderly woman, who I take it was the head of sales, approached us addressing Miss Hyland formally by name.

"There's no racks," I commented as I gazed quizzically around the room. Except for a couple of small rosewood stands the space consisted of a couch, two Queen Anne chairs, a glass coffee table, and a pair of end tables.

"Would you two care to take a seat?" offered the sales woman graciously, indicating the small couch. "May we get you anything, coffee, tea, dessert?"

Miss Hyland looked at her wristwatch, an expensive Gruen with a diamond band.

"I believe I have an appointment for a fitting in 10 minutes," she replied. "Would it be possible for us to be alone until then?"

A curtained doorway near the center of the room parted and a live mannequin stepped out dressed in a cobalt blue, silk evening gown. At Miss Hyland's request the elder sales lady waved the model away, very soon following suit through the same exit. Finally alone, we approached the couch.

"You were not straight with me," I began once we were seated. "Why didn't you tell me you were being blackmailed?"

"It's something I am not proud of," she replied simply.

"If you expect me to protect you, I have to have all the facts!"

"How did you get those photographs?"

"Let's say we were able to tap your blackmailer's resources."

"Do you know who it is?"

"Say, who's asking the questions around here?" I scolded. "Now are you going to fill me in on the details, or not?"

"Very well," she surrendered.

Staring down at the glass coffee table she related her story, sometimes speaking in barely a whisper.

"You know my background. Rich girl spoiled by her daddy's indulgences. I wanted to shed that image and, against my father's wishes, started looking into ways of making it on my own and creating some real purpose to my life. He particularly wasn't happy when I chose the entertainment industry. 'Gypsies,' he called them, and said that at one time 'they weren't even welcomed into boarding houses!' He relented, however, with the stipulation that I remain living at home and keep my association with fellow colleagues on a business level. 'Hyland's do not socialize with Hollywood types. It wouldn't do for our family's standing, and particularly for the image of our business!'" She then added as a quick aside, "As if anyone who drank Hyland milk really cared if I got in before midnight or not!"

"But obviously someone thought they did!" I commented.

"Yes," she replied, sadly. "I made a mistake, and now I'm paying dearly for it." She leaned forward and cradled her head in her hands. "Dad was always good to me. We traveled everywhere, especially after my mother's death. This one time, however... I think he was taking a tour of China... I wasn't able to go with him. I'd just started working at the studio and was smack in the middle of a picture, so I couldn't take the time off."

"How long ago was that?" I asked interrupting.

"About ten months ago. We had an awful row about it, right up until the time that he'd left. And then perhaps a day or two later, I was invited to one of those Hollywood parties. You know like the ones that you read about in those photoplay magazines. My friends at the studio were giving me a hard time because I initially refused to attend. And I don't know whether it was because of their dares, or perhaps that I was feeling a little rebellious, or even just plain lonely, but eventually I gave in and went…"

"Who was putting it on?".

"Jack Clemmons. It was at his house in the Hollywood Hills. His wife was away and I guess he just felt like sowing some oats. Everyone from the studio was invited, and although everything started out all prim and proper, as the evening wore on things started getting out of hand. There were some drugs and some quality bootlegged gin, which loosened everyone up a bit. I thought I could handle it… well, I guess those pictures proves otherwise."

"Do you recall any of the events later that evening?"

"I'm afraid not. One minute I was sipping gin and the next I woke up on the living room floor with no memory of what happened."

"Not even when you played mermaid in the pool?"

"I can't remember even going near the pool, let alone…"

Here her voice faded out as she shook her head sorrowfully.

"Well, it seemed someone at that gathering was handy with a camera," I reflected, "…*perhaps too conveniently handy.*"

"You're suggesting that it was a frame up?"

"Pretty evident, wouldn't you say? It wouldn't take much to drop a 'Mickey' in your drink, undress you, and snap a few photos."

She acted surprised. Either she was a good actress, or exceedingly naïve. At the moment, I wasn't sure which. I then asked, "What happened next?"

"Nothing. I went home thinking it was all a little strange, and didn't realize the extent of my trouble until I was contacted by the blackmailer about a week later. It was then that I saw a copy of one of those photographs and realized the fix I was in!"

"Did you have any idea who might be blackmailing you? Even a guess?"

"I have no idea whatsoever... not even a clue. I just paid as I was instructed; leaving an envelope with the cash at the different locations specified, and then walking away without looking back." Her next words sounded more desperate, "Look, I had no choice. If these photos get out I know it will kill my poor father!"

"You don't think that Geary might be involved in some way...that perhaps she might have been working with the blackmailer... or was the blackmailer herself?"

"Impossible," she responded emphatically.

"Why?"

"I...I, couldn't believe it of her," she answered, faltering for an answer. "Besides, she wasn't at Clemmons' party."

"But, that still doesn't rule her out as being somehow involved."

She had to agree.

I'd one more question to ask of my client and a pivotal one. "That note you showed me on the first day at my office, was it real?"

She seemed suddenly taken aback; I wasn't sure if it was the question or the blunt way in which I framed it. She responded, "Real, of course!"

Her next action told me that she was becoming extremely uncomfortable with the direction of the conversation. Rising suddenly she asked to be excused, supposedly to visit the little girl's room. She was gone for some time, and when she returned I could tell that she'd regained some of her composure.

"I'm sorry," she said, once again taking a seat next to me. "Where were we…oh, yes we were talking about the note. It was definitely real!"

"Then how do you see it fitting into all this?" I asked. "As I recall it threatened your life if you talked. If it was referring to the fact that you were being blackmailed it wouldn't make any sense. The only person made vulnerable by that piece of information being released would be you…" I paused for a moment as a thought suddenly struck me. "Unless the blackmailer thought that you suspected his or her identity."

"That could be a possibility, but they'd be wrong. As I'd mentioned earlier, I can't even imagine who might be doing this to me."

"Well, it's a thought anyway."

I got up from the couch, and started to leave. As I took a few paces I turned, adding, "Think hard and let me know if you come up with any names that might come to you."

"I'll be here for at least another hour. You can ask my driver to take you to wherever you need to go. Just tell him he needs to be back here by three." I took another couple of steps toward the door when her hail stopped me dead in my tracks. "Logan, about those pictures…"

"Don't worry," I said patting my jacket pocket. "They're safe right where they are for now."

Clemmons initially wasn't anxious to leave his meeting to talk with me, but when I hinted at the reason for my unexpected visit he immediately announced a fifteen minute break to those gathered in the conference room, and directed me swiftly to his private office. Once I told him that I saw his blackmailer's accusations he started singing like Caruso.

"They're unfounded, you know," he said once he settled into a chair behind his desk. "The paternity accusations are all a bunch of hogwash."

"There was a mention of infidelity," I corrected. "I didn't see anything regarding paternity."

"Well, that's come up in the last three months."

"But do you deny the infidelity charge?"

"Look, I'm going to be frank…medically it's impossible for me to father kids," he answered straightforwardly, yet ignoring my last question. "Something to do with my sperm count."

"But, again," I pressed, "was the infidelity charge unfounded?"

"No," he finally admitted. "And that is the only reason why I paid…that, and to avoid the inevitable publicity that might be generated. In our business scandals can be deadly."

"I know this next question may seem un-gentlemanly, but it has to be asked if I'm to get at the truth. Who was the lady in question?"

He paused, reluctant at first to answer, but finally making up his mind said, "Fran Adams. It was a casual affair, going off and on for the past six months. It started on the night I held a party at my home when my wife was away. We were discreet. I just can't figure out how someone found out."

"Do you think Miss Geary heard anything along those lines?"

"I beg your pardon?"

"Women talk among themselves," I explained. "Do you think Adams may have mentioned it to Geary?"

"I have no way of knowing. I guess it's possible… why?" He suddenly caught on to what I was implying:

"You're not suggesting that Geary was the blackmailer?"

"I'm not saying one way or the other," I answered as noncommittally as possible. "But now that we've brought up the subject... what's your thoughts?"

He paused for a second. "Well the last time I was contacted..." Here I interrupted.

"When was that?"

"A couple of weeks ago." I nodded my head and then indicated that he continue. "The last time I was contacted, it came directly from the blackmailer. In the past, notes usually showed up with drop instructions... but only in this last communication did I receive a phone call directly from the blackmailer. It was a male voice, obviously disguised... So," he finally concluded, "I think that would eliminate Geary."

I was going to respond with the same observation I'd made to Hyland in regards to her conclusion of Geary's innocence, when he suddenly added something interesting. "There was also another thing different this time around. He made an unusual request... all the other times it was cash... but this time he wanted my movie script."

"What did you make of that?" I asked quickly.

"In the beginning," he continued, "I thought that the blackmailer was planning to sell it. Perhaps he already had a buyer. Other studios or the press will pay big dough for something like that. You know, inside information. But after you mentioned your client's threatening note at lunch the other day, I started to realize that it might've been for a more sinister purpose...and that scared me. I wasn't sure what that would get me involved in."

I told him for the moment I was through with his questioning, but requested the use of his office for a while longer. He agreed and I asked that he send in Taylor.

"So the cat's out of the bag!" Taylor announced entering the room. "Before you ask, I heard it from Mattie. She called me awhile ago." That explained the sudden visit to the ladies room at Bullocks Wilshire. "Look, I have to apologize," he continued. "It was my idea, not Mattie's, to keep that information from you. I really didn't think at the time that it was necessary to embarrass the girl any further by revealing that she was being blackmailed... or especially for her having to explain the existence of those photos."

"As gallant as that may be, don't you think it was a little foolish?" I replied. "How could I deal with a blackmail case if I wasn't told that it was one from the beginning."

"I'm afraid I didn't think it through properly. The note was what got us to act; otherwise we may have still been dragging our feet."

"How long was she being blackmailed?"

"About ten months."

"And when did she confide in you?"

"I'd say at least four, maybe five months ago."

"And you waited that long before getting help."

"As I said, it was the note that made us act."

I decided it was time to drop the other shoe.

"I guess you're aware that I have the photos." He nodded. "Aren't you curious where I got them?"

Here he looked slightly uncomfortable, and after a minute of reflection responded, "You're going to tell me that whatever the source of that information was, you learned that I'm being blackmailed as well?"

"True," I responded, studying his face carefully.

"Did this source say exactly why I was being black-mailed?" he returned with the same searching gaze.

"Perhaps you can tell me." I don't know if it was my imagination, but my answer seemed to have noticeably put him at ease.

"As you recall I'm a married man," he quickly explained. "I believe I'd explained these circumstances when I'd hired you six months ago. But in any case, I'll relate it again:

"I walked out on my wife, Connie, about two years ago when I moved out to the west coast. I was employed as an editor at a studio in Jersey for about nine months when I got this offer to become an assistant director at Champion Studios. We weren't getting along all too well beforehand, but after I accepted the job the marriage really hit the rocks. When the time came for me to begin work, I just took off; 'abandonment,' I believe they call it.

"Well, after being separated about a year and a half, she served me papers. The divorce proceedings were just beginning when I got caught up in that Badger scheme, and unfortunately is still in the works today, except of late they've become even nastier. I couldn't afford to be caught up in a scandal back then, and I certainly can't now… especially with her lawyers breathing down my neck. Back then it was a clear case of frame up; however this time I really am romantically involved with another woman and unfortunately the blackmailer has found me out."

"I assume you wouldn't want to supply that woman's name."

"I think you can guess," he responded with a knowing smile. "However, if you want to check up on my story I can supply the name of my wife's lawyers."

I told him that I did. And after he'd jotted it down on a scrap of paper, I asked, "What method did the blackmailer use to contact you?"

"Before I answer that," he replied, "aren't you curious what was asked of me?" I nodded, and he continued, "You were questioning me earlier about employing Geary. I lied to you. The only reason I'd interest in the girl was because it was part of the agreement. In exchange for keeping the affair quiet I was to use my influence to find continual employment for her."

"Didn't you find that strange?" I asked.

"Not if Geary was somehow involved with the blackmailer."

That would be a logical conclusion. I returned to my original question, "And what about method of contact?"

"*This*," he said with a gleam in his eye, "you might find interesting. I just heard from the blackmailer this morning. He wants my script, and asked that I leave it at a specified drop point. Care to come along and witness it for yourself?"

17

TWO MURDERS IN ONE NIGHT

What goes through the mind of a killer? What kind of emotion, if any, does he feel: fear, guilt, or elation? These thoughts caused me to further ask the question, "What sort of a killer was I up against?" He was cold and calculating, that much so far has been true. But what was driving him? Would he strike again? And ultimately, will I be able to stop him?

Taylor explained that the blackmailer had called him at his office, instructing that his script be left in substitute for his previous services as Geary's employer. That function was understandably no longer of any value, which necessitated a change in the bargaining chips.

"What did his voice sound like?" I asked.

"It was male, but muffled," he replied thinking hard. "I'm sure he was trying to disguise it."

"And what were his instructions?"

"He said I was to take my script, wrap it in newspaper, and leave it at the edge of the Santa Monica Pier before seven tonight."

"Did you ask him why your script?"

"He didn't give me a chance," he replied shortly. "He just gave the instructions and hung up."

Once again the blackmailer was requesting a script, but logically it didn't make any sense. The first had already served its purpose, so why the need for a second? And even if the first script had been destroyed or lost, there are other sources like newspapers and magazines to get the materials necessary for the construction of another letter… assuming that would be its purpose. What value then was Taylor's script? I decided this was another mystery that hopefully would become clearer in time.

I tried reaching Soames at home by telephone. He was the only person left that I hadn't followed up on. Rita had his number on file. At first the line was busy, and when I tried again later it just kept ringing. Was he gone, or was he just not taking any calls?

I met Taylor at six and taking one of the studio's cars we drove to the pier. The journey took us along

Sunset to La Cienega, and then west on Santa Monica Boulevard to the beach. By the time we arrived, the ocean was bathed in the last glow of the day. Orange, red, and yellow rays creating an ever changing light show that reflected off the water in flashes of glittering white sparkles, and settling as a warm golden glow over the pristine sand. Parking the car along the Roosevelt Highway, we took a short walk to the Municipal Pier which ran adjacent to the boardwalk. This boardwalk was the same one that Clancy and I had visited last week. It was now 6:45 as Taylor and I strolled along the 1,600 foot-long walkway that was held suspended above the tranquil waters of the Pacific. By agreement we separated and I kept my distance, walking well behind, keenly observing the immediate surroundings as we sauntered along.

The pier was surprisingly deserted, even for mid-week. It made my job of shadowing Taylor easy. Eventually I selected a secure observation area that was located by the railing alongside a tall cement beam. Here I stopped and leaned against a pillar. Taylor, I observed, was still taking his time reaching the end of the pier. With package tucked securely under one arm, he eventually reached the drop point and, as unpretentiously as possible, placed the package at his feet. Working it neatly with his foot, he pushed it behind a large post. He stalled a moment longer, presumably to light a cigarette, and then satisfied, walked quickly away.

It didn't take long for something to happen. Almost the instant that he left, I heard an engine from a motor boat roar suddenly to life. Seeking it out, I caught sight of the craft speeding by me about twenty feet away. Smith was at the wheel and he was directing it toward the end of the pier. Looking back along the walkway I could see an iron ladder running down the piling and terminating at the water's edge. Quickly surmising that it was his objective, I started toward it. But, before I could take a dozen steps, Taylor suddenly appeared out of nowhere brandishing a gun and waving it wildly.

"You bastard," he cried out. "You murdering bastard!" he shouted again as he fired off several shots in the direction of the motor boat. By the time I reached him, he was crouched by the rail frantically reloading. I tried to talk some sense into him, but he was acting strange, almost like a man completely out of control. He stood up again to fire, and I tried to pull him down. Like a fool, he was unduly exposing himself to return fire. I started to break cover in a last ditch effort to get a firmer grip on his shoulder, when the sharp crack of a handgun suddenly arrested my effort and sent me diving back onto the deck. From my position lying flat against the rough planks, I looked up in horror as a red stain blossomed like a poinsettia across the front of his white shirt. Gripping his chest, Taylor stood momentarily unsteady, his body rocking from side to side before abruptly lurching forward and pitching itself over the railing and into the sea.

I immediately looked for Smith, but saw that he was out of range and speeding away. Quickly removing my shoes and jacket, I leapt over the side in Taylor's wake. I hit the water so hard that my breath was immediately taken from me, and I floundered for a second before I could get my bearings. It was dark, cold, and dangerous, and I couldn't see a thing. Several times I had to swim against the current to avoid the pull of the waves, which were constantly trying to slap me back against the cement pilings. The last time they almost succeeded and in the process I gasped and swallowed some water. Choking, I broke the surface and instantly felt hands reaching out for me.

"There's someone else down there!" I cried as they heaved me into the small narrow row boat and wrapped me in some warm blankets.

"We know," someone said. "There's another boat looking for him now."

"It was Smith all right," I told Red later over a cup of hot coffee in his office. I'd called him at home and he'd met me at police headquarters, arriving just as I'd finished making a statement to the silver-haired sergeant at the front desk.

"And ya not sure dat it was his double?"

I sighed. "No, Red. *I'm not sure.* It was growing dark; he was some distance away; and quite truthfully all I saw was the jacket, hat, and red scarf." I took a long swallow of the hot liquid and felt it warm my insides. Although my clothes were now dry, my body still felt chilled. "Have they found Taylor yet?"

"No, but it's only been a couple of hours. Da tide's going out now. If they don't find him, I expect he might wash up on a beach somewhere in da next couple of days." He took a sip of his own coffee, and then asked, "By da way, were you able to get a shot off at dat rascal?"

"It happened pretty fast. I didn't even get my gun out of my holster. Which reminds me, you wouldn't happen to have a kit around? I need to get the Pacific Ocean out of my Colt."

He reached into his drawer and pulled out a brush and cloth. As I set about going thoroughly over my weapon under the light of his desk lamp, we continued our conversation.

"So it looks like we could scratch one suspect," he commented after a long pause.

"So it seems," I replied, while running the narrow brush around the barrel.

"What did you find out from da others?"

"Both Clemmons and Hyland admitted to the blackmailer's charges. I guess in Hyland's case she really didn't have any option. Clemmons finally came clean about his script and said it was part of a recent deal, and…"

I was about to tell him about Taylor's marital problems, which I guess now was literally a dead issue, when I was interrupted by the ringing of Red's phone. He picked it up and after a brief exchange replaced the receiver firmly on its cradle.

"Are you about done with dat gun?" he said with an edge of excitement that suddenly roused my interest. "You may need it!"

"I can be. Why?"

"Dat was Vice. They've just got an anonymous tip about a drug deal dat's planned for tonight."

"So, what's that have to do with us?"

"The buyer in question is none other than our suspect, Dick Soames. But let's not waste time," he said gathering his jacket. "The boys in Vice are already heading out. We better get a move on."

That explained why I wasn't able to reach Soames earlier, I thought to myself as I reached for my hat.

Heading toward the rendezvous point I learned from Red that an unidentified male had called Vice and informed them that a drug deal was about to take place. He gave the time: 10:00 p.m., location: parking lot Hollywood Bowl, and specifically mentioned Soames by name. The caller also suggested that Inspector Clancy be notified and hung up. The last bit was particularly curious and raised some unsettling questions.

The Hollywood Bowl was a band shell built in a natural amphitheater formerly called Daisy Dell. It was opened in 1922 and has been the official summer home of the Los Angeles Philharmonic ever since. Seating, located along the hillside of Bolton Canyon, faces down toward a stage which is surrounded by distinctive concentric arches forming a shell. Just last season architects built a new covering using a hard composite material, which unfortunately by recent reports was not delivering the enhanced acoustics as did the earlier structure.

Red pulled the car into an empty lot across from the Bowl and cut the lights. In the darkness I could just make out three other unmarked cars parked next to each other. A small group of about twelve officers were gathered receiving orders. We joined them.

"I need four of you," the commanding officer was instructing, "to cover the area just west of the main entrance, another east, and one central unit for a frontal advance. I need at least one man covering both of the exits, the main lot and Odin Street, and one man each circling to the rear of our suspects. On my signal… one long sound from my car horn… those of you who are not covering the driveways advance toward the two automobiles now parked near the entrance. Be cautious, we don't know if they're armed. It looks like we are up against three men, so it should be a walk in the park, but still take every precaution not to be seen. Do not use your weapons unless you absolutely have to."

He looked around. "OK?" They all nodded. "Then let's move out!"

Red and I followed the central unit. A couple of the plain clothes officers had shotguns while the other two uniformed men had their handguns out. I glanced along Highland and noticed two parked unmarked cars both facing the entrance, but from opposite ends of the block, each containing I would guess at least two officers.

There were no performances that evening and the parking lot was isolated and dark; perfect for the crime that was about to take place. It took some time for my eyes to get adjusted but, as we silently crossed Highland Avenue to the edge of the lot, I could see two late-model sedans parked facing each other just off to the left of the main entrance.

Two of the men did not look familiar, but the third was definitely Soames. We hunkered down and waited for the signal from the commander. One that wouldn't come until he was sure all his men were properly in position. Several long minutes passed before it sounded, the continuous blast of a car horn that he'd promised, and then we all closed in with one big rush. Both police cars came tearing along Highland skidding to a stop, effectively blocking the entrance, their headlights suddenly illuminating the scene. The two cars, the drug dealers, and Soames could now be clearly seen. At first the three men started to run, but realizing that they were surrounded and outnumbered, threw their hands up in surrender as the officers began moving in. It was then that the shot rang out and I saw Soames crumble to the ground.

Confusion soon followed, accompanied by additional gunshots and cries. And by the time we were finally given the "all clear," and could make our way to the body, Soames was dead.

We were still not sure what had exactly gone wrong as Red drove me back to my apartment. At least the unofficial debriefing at the scene brought to light two pieces of information: That none of the officers had claimed firing that first shot, and a few reported that it sounded like it may have come from a shotgun.

Early the next morning Red found a deserted desk in a corner of the Homicide Division for me. The toxicology reports had returned and confirmed what we had suspected. Geary was drugged. They found traces of the chemical *Chloral Hydrate* in her bloodstream and stomach contents. To my mind the mode of entry was undoubtedly the coffee she was drinking, which brought up the next question. Why would it be necessary to sedate her prior to the murder?

"Too bad I didn't get to Soames sooner," I said to myself. "He might've cleared up that little mystery."

"What's dat?" Red asked, overhearing me.

"Sorry," I replied, "I guess I was thinking aloud. I was wondering about Soames. I wouldn't be surprised if he hadn't supplied the *Chloral Hydrate* that spiked Geary's coffee. From what we know now, he had the sources."

"It was marijuana dat he was after last night according to da reports coming out of Vice," Red added. "But ya could be right. I'm sure he could have gotten his hands on any drug…legal or illegal."

"And, I might even take this further," I continued reasoning, "If the pattern holds up…Clemmons and Taylor were 'touched' for specific purposes that somehow fits into some grand scheme of the blackmailer; Clemmons, the script, and Taylor, Geary's employment. Therefore, it could also follow that Soames may have been used in a similar manner by providing the drug for Geary's coffee."

"And what about Hyland?" Red asked.

"She's the only one who's being hit hard in the cash department. We saw that from Geary's ledger. However," I added thoughtfully, "I'll question her later. Maybe something more is being asked of her."

"I'll also talk to Vice," Red offered. "Maybe they can get a lead on some of Soames' contacts."

"Any luck reaching Adams' parents?" I asked, suddenly realizing that the hairdresser was the only source that we really hadn't tapped yet.

"No," he replied simply, "but I'll keep on it."

I returned my attention back to the papers I had on my desk. Amongst them I discovered a report on the prints from the bottle and glass I had given Red earlier in the week. After routing this evidence through the Bureau of Investigation and various state and local law enforcement agencies, the Records Department was now able to provide me with a name and complete background on the individual who had been calling himself Smith. In light of Taylor's murder the previous night, I was especially interested to learn about this individual. I started reading. Smith's true name was Victorio Aldo Rappo. He was born and raised in New York City's Little Italy district on March 9, 1901. By his early youth he had gained the reputation of a street thug; and by his late teens became a member of the Masseria Mob. He had risen quickly in their ranks, eventually becoming lieutenant to its leader, Giuseppe "Joe the Boss" Masseria, and was exceptionally effective as an enforcer during the prolonged turf war with the rival crime boss Salvatore Maranzano. Charles "Lucky" Luciano joined on about this time, and convinced Masseria to send Rappo off to California with an eye on setting up a West Coast connection. It was thought that Luciano wasn't so much interested in expanding the business as getting his competition, Rappo, out of the way. As Luciano grew in power, Rappo decided to step aside, voluntarily leaving the mob on his own locomotion instead of the other option… feet first.

I thumbed past the rest of the biographic material for the present and examined the photos with the physical descriptions attached alongside. Aside for a few extra pounds and a change in hair color, it was our man. Another detail I came across that cemented the I.D. was a note scribbled across the bottom of one of the reports. It said: Victorio Aldo Rappo, aka Vic "the Reptile" Rappo. It was not known if he was called that because of his cold-blooded mannerisms, or because he had a condition of hypothyroidism that left him continually feeling cold, even in warm weather. He was also known to wear scarves, presumably to cover a six-inch scar that ran from the back of his left ear to the center of his Adam's apple; the result of a stiletto blade yielded by an opponent during a fight in his youth.

I turned another page and started reading of his more recent activities. When I saw that he had taken up with a Dean Gioani, a sudden bell went off inside. Gioani was the man I helped put away a little over six months ago. He was running that Badger racket that Taylor had gotten caught up in. Coincidence, or was a pattern starting to form here?

I tried to remember the particulars of that case. I'd recalled that two people were specifically involved in the con: Gioani and a girl whom he'd used to set up the victim or "mark" as they call him. The Badger game incidentally was an extortion scheme usually perpetrated on married men, who were tricked into a compromising position with a lady for the purpose of blackmail.

A third man, Rappo, was mentioned in association with Gioani and the girl, but he apparently had been out of the country at the time of the crime and so little concern to my case. I did see a photograph of him then, and that was probably what caused the feeling of 'déjà vu' that night in my office when I finally got a look at him. I had to search my memory in regards to the girl.

She had been in court during the trial, testifying as the D.A.'s witness. A plea deal saved her from doing time in prison.

Another thought hit me.

"Red," I called nearly startling him out of his chair. "You have those autopsy photos of Geary?"

"Sure, why?"

"I just have a wild hunch," I replied. "Can I see them?" Red went into the file cabinet and removed a folder. I had only seen a partial view of Geary's face as she had lain face down on the floor. And even then it was a mess. I figured these photos could provide a better look.

"Yes…" I said studying it. "*It's just possible!* The hair is cut and bleached, and she has lost some weight…" And something else struck me. The description of the gangster with Geary at the talent agency also tallies with Gioani's. So there is a connection!

"What are you mumbling about, Thomas?"

I thought frantically for a second and finally came up with a name. "Red get onto Records and see if they have anything on a Bridget O'Malley."

"O'Malley," he repeated, and quickly wrote it down.

"Yes. There should be something in connection with that Gioani case from about six months ago. Specifically ask for any photos."

"Why? Have you seen a ghost?"

"I just may have, Red…," I said with some satisfaction. *"I just may have!"*

18

A SECOND WARNING

A jungle cat survives because it uses its senses. A prey doesn't have to approach too closely before a cat's sharp perceptions will turn it into a scrumptious meal, laid out nicely upon the feline's plate. It pays to learn from nature, especially in my business. To keep one's eyes and ears open is something of a "must." Keen observation and the ability to listen always pay far reaching dividends, especially toward the solution of a case.

I t was around 9:00 a.m. when I finished with the reports. My head was spinning. The information was coming in fast and furious, and I was trying to piece it all together. I asked Red to get onto the powers that be at San Quentin prison and see if we could get access to Gioani. Maybe the department could send a couple of boys, or better yet set up an interview over the telephone.

I was anxious to get Gioani's take on both Rappo and O'Malley, and time was of the essence. Regarding contacting Adams' parents, Red still wasn't having any luck, and I suggested that he call the Santa Barbara Sheriff's Department and see if they could look into it; perhaps even send a car over to the house.

I'd started to leave the office when Red's phone started ringing off the hook. As I reached the door, I turned and saw that he was making frantic motions for me to wait. He spoke urgently for a few minutes and then waved me over.

"I just got a call from Central. They said that Mr. Hyland just phoned requesting dat police come to his estate immediately. He has received a threatening note addressed to his daughter." He then added as an afterthought, "Are ya interested in checking it out?"

"I think I'd better," I replied thoughtfully. "I wonder if this is some new note, or has he somehow stumbled onto the old one?"

Before I left the office I specifically instructed Red that if he heard anything regarding Adams' whereabouts he was to call me immediately.

He agreed.

I hitched a ride with one of his detectives, a young man named Vince Scalletti, and we drove out in an unmarked car to the estate in Bel Air. Mr. Hyland was surprised to see me when he greeted us in the foyer of the mansion.

"I didn't know you were with the police. As I recall, Mattie said you were a private investigator looking into that business at the studio."

"Actually, I am. But I'm also working with the police. They asked me to come along when they got your call. They figured it might somehow tie into the studio investigation."

That was only part of the story. I purposely left off mentioning the first threatening note his daughter received, and how this new one might tie into it. I was still trying to respect my client's wishes, and keep that particular information from him.

He showed us into an enormous den, paneled in rich oak, polished to a luster, and carpeted with expensive Persian rugs and black leather furniture. Various plaques and awards lay strewn about the room, with some of the more important ones displayed in glass cases; and on three of the walls hung mounted animal heads. I asked him about these, and he'd said that they were not purchased, but actual trophies of the hunt. He had killed them on safari in India. The final wall space was taken up by a large floor to ceiling bookcase crammed with expensively bound books. There were also a large number of personal photographs, obviously taken either on trips or during special events. Almost all of them had him standing next to his daughter.

One particularly stood out, a photograph of the two of them standing next to President Hoover. Hyland led us to a large desk and picked up a sheet of paper.

"I found it this morning," he said handing it to me. "It was sitting here on my blotter."

It was, at a glance, similar to the first note. The words were cut out and pasted onto a sheet of paper to form a message; but there were two very significant differences. Instead of just warning her to keep her mouth shut as in the first, it instructed her to leave the studio and not associate with any of its staff again. The consequence of disobedience was stated as death, and it even addressed Miss Hyland by her first name. The second variance was the stock of paper that was used. Whereas the first was put together using expensive stationary, this was nothing more than cheap typing paper.

"Any idea who might've left it?" I asked, handing it over to Scalletti so he could get a closer look.

"Not really. It could have been one of the staff. It was mixed in with the rest of my morning mail."

"Have you questioned them?" Scalletti asked.

"I checked with those here, and they claim to know nothing about it. However two of my staff are out shopping… the cook and a maid. I'll ask them when they return."

"Was there an envelope?"

"Yes." He handed it to me. It was post marked two days ago from a post office in San Bernardino County.

The address was typed and there was no return. I handed it to Scalletti. It, along with the note, had now become police property.

As I turned back toward Mr. Hyland, a gilded framed photograph on his desk caught my eye. He followed my stare.

"My daughter and I are very close," he said with a noticeable depth of emotion. He picked up the photograph and gazed at it lovingly. It was an attractive portrait of her. She was dressed in an expensive silk formal with quarter length sleeves and trimmed in lace. She wore make-up, but only minimally, and her golden hair was swept up to expose a long, swan-like neck adorned with a necklace of sparkling diamonds. Her father stood proudly next to her in the photo, looking smart in his tailored tux, his arm wrapped tightly about her shoulders. Both displayed wide grins and a joyous glint in their eyes. Obviously these two people were enjoying life and embraced the world of wealth which they were fortunate enough to be a part of, especially during these unusually hard times.

I watched as he stared for some moments with contentment at the photograph, and then suddenly, just as a cloud overshadows a pastoral setting, his eyes darkened.

"If anyone," he said with surprising intensity, "even thinks about harming my daughter, I will shoot them dead."

"Not a wise choice of words," Scalletti interjected.

An uncomfortable moment followed which I attempted to break. "That's a nice photograph of the two of you," I began. "Were you at some special function?"

It worked.

"Yes. It was taken the Sunday before last at the 'Founder's Ball.'"

At that moment something odd struck me, but I hadn't time to dwell on it, for the phone had rung and, after a short pause, the butler came in to announce that it was for me from an Inspector Clancy. I took it on the extension in the entrance hall. Before I could even finish saying hello, Red blurted out on the other end, "We've located her!"

"Adams?" I asked.

"Naw, J. Edgar Hoover!" Red commented sarcastically. "Of course, Adams…are ya losing it, me boy!"

"No, I was just being sure. Where is she?" I returned evenly.

"Lake Arrowhead," he replied. "I called her parents one last time before trying to reach da sheriff's department… they'd just got back from meeting her at the lake. It seems they had the key to the family cabin."

That explained the reference to 'Key C' on her calendar; 'Key to Cabin.'

Red continued, "They were extremely cautious at first before giving da information. It took some convincing that she was in need of police protection… and I had them call me back at H.Q. to establish that I was genuine… after dat they opened up."

"You told them not to try and contact her," I interrupted anxiously. "She could go on the lam again."

"Give me some credit, Thomas! I wasn't promoted to detective because I have a pretty face."

"If that was the case you'd still be walking a beat," I shot back. "OK, give me the location of the cabin and anything else you might have."

He did. And when he'd concluded, I asked that he get onto someone from the county sheriff's department and ask that they stake out the cabin. I then added in closing, "Tell them not to get too close… just keep tabs. We don't want to spook her."

As he hung up I heard a noise on the line. I said hello and the butler answered. He said he was just hanging up the extension's receiver. I accepted his excuse, but it still left me wondering.

I lingered long enough to make a show of investigating the note, and then made my excuses to Mr. Hyland. It wasn't as though I thought that the threat shouldn't be taken seriously, but considering the direction of my investigation as of late, reaching Fran Adams still seemed pretty important.

We were just leaving, walking over to the car, when Miss Hyland came running toward us. She was coming up a path that led from the garage. As she reached us she stumbled, dropping her purse. We helped her replace the spilled contents, the usual items; lipstick, glasses, brush, and comb. Breathless she asked, "Did Father show you the note?"

"Yes," I said, "but what are you doing here?"

"Father called me at the studio," she answered. "I came as fast as I could." Here she lowered her voice and leaned closer to my ear, "You didn't mention the earlier note, did you?" I said no, and she seemed relieved. "I'm afraid, Logan," she continued. "Could you stay with me?" I told her it was impossible, but she pleaded all the more, "I'll pay well for your protection. I don't feel safe... even here in my own home. Remember one attempt was already made on my life!"

"You'll be OK," I said trying to calm her. "Just stay indoors."

She still seemed nervous, so I asked Scalletti to remain behind and guard her. Miss Hyland wasn't totally satisfied with this arrangement, and I had to convince the detective that it would be OK. I would take responsibility for the change in plans and promised to notify his boss, Red about his new assignment.

I pulled the Ford into the nearest service station and told the attendant to fill it up. The price had recently risen to .17 per gallon. However, feeling like a big spender, I decided to pull out all the stops and top the tank off. Besides, being that this was police business I could charge it to the department's account. While the car was being fueled I walked over to the office and helped myself to a map, and then asked the cashier, flashing my I.D, for the use of his phone. He agreed, and I put a call through to Homicide.

Red wasn't pleased that I had left Scalletti behind, but agreed that it was my only option. He said that he would send a replacement to act as my backup, and that this detective would meet me at the lake.

I got onto the highway and eventually left L.A., passing amongst acres of bountiful orange groves whose dark green leaves and colorful fruit always reminded me of my vision of Eden. In the distance I could see the surrounding San Gabriel Mountains, looming purple against the afternoon haze. This range of mountains is made up of a number of peaks. Most notably Mt. Wilson which at 5,715 feet is the home of the Mount Wilson Observatory. Back when it was built in 1908, it had the largest operational telescope in the world; and Mt. San Antonio, commonly referred to as Mt. Baldy, the highest point in Los Angeles County topping out at 10,068 feet.

It was a hot day and I had my window rolled down. A scent of citrus drifted in on the breeze and filled the car with its distinctive fruity odor. At one point I pulled over at a stand advertising freshly squeezed juice, using the stop as an excuse to watch passing cars and to confirm that I wasn't being tailed. Perhaps I was being paranoid, but I couldn't shake that incident with the butler. It was still hanging like some ominous shadow in the back of my mind. Once satisfied, I continued on my journey that soon exchanged the countryside from groves to dairies. Here, I wondered if Hyland had some pastures. There was certainly plenty of land for it and a lot of roaming milk cows. During the trip I consulted my map several times, and it pretty much guided me successfully past the crossroads until I finally connected with the final highway that would snake up the San Bernardino Mountains. Some forty-five miles of winding road that would eventually lead me to the lake.

Lake Arrowhead is located 80 miles from Los Angeles and some 5,108 ft. above sea level. Nestled in the San Bernardino Mountains amongst a pine forest, this beautiful, blue, pristine lake helped earn the resort the title of "Alps of Southern California." The lake itself is 1.5 miles wide and 2.2 miles in length with a shoreline of 14 miles and a depth of 185 ft. It's a favorite vacation spot for Angelenos, including celebrities such as Howard Hughes, Charles Lindbergh, and Mae West, who've been frequent guests at 'The Raven,' a three-story, English tavern style lodge. Built in 1917, it has twenty-eight rooms with views of the surrounding 100-year-old cedars and tall, majestic pines. I drove by this lodge as I directed the car through the entrance to the village.

They weren't obvious, but as I neared the location of the Adams' cabin I spotted two sheriff's car and at least four officers that had taken up watch in the vicinity. I immediately pulled up and identified myself.

They pointed out the cabin. It was rustic in appearance, a two-story affair constructed out of milled ponderosa pine logs set on a cement foundation, with a roof of pine and cedar shingles. A covered porch ran the length of the front, accessed by climbing three wooden steps which also led directly up to a broad wooden front door. There were medium sized windows on both floors framed by wooden louvers that were painted a dark olive green. A large chimney of cut granite stone jutted up from the right side of the building, and fieldstones of this same component could also be found accenting various elements on the exterior walls.

The cabin itself was set back on a dirt lot that was surrounded by pines and situated only a couple of yards from the lake. The grounds were fairly bare except for fallen pine needles and a few wildflowers growing in some primitive rock planter boxes running along the base of the porch. It looked quiet, but a thin wisp of blue smoke was coming from the chimney.

"Have you seen any activity?" I asked a tall, thin, gray haired man who had identified himself as the county sheriff; Bradshaw by name.

"We haven't seen any movement at all… at least not since we arrived," he consulted his watch, "which was about an hour and a half ago."

"I'm waiting on a detective from Los Angeles," I explained. "He can't be too far behind. When he arrives we'll move in on the cabin."

As I uttered those instructions I happened to glance back toward the cabin. From the corner of my eye I caught the glint of a blue flash appearing in one of the upper story windows. It was followed almost simultaneously by the unmistakable sound of a muffled shot.

19

A TRAIL OF DEATH

There comes a time in one's day-to-day existence where you eventually have to face your Waterloo. It's never a pleasant affair, but usually can be tolerated if you accept it as just another of life's hard knocks. Nevertheless, in my business certain situations don't allow for passiveness. Lying down and playing dead is never an option. To go so far as to accept defeat could nine times out of ten spell disaster, or even death. My philosophy is if you have to go down, do so swinging. Just like Davy Crockett up there on the walls of the Alamo, using ole Betsy as a club as wave upon wave of the enemy came at him. He never gave up nor relinquished any ground until his last breath was spent. "Action not apathy" is my motto, and let the epitaph on my tombstone read: "He never gave up, and went down fighting."

As soon as we heard the shot we ducked for cover, drawing our weapons. Using the trunk of a tree for protection, I watched as the sheriff, who was crouched nearby, used hand signals to silently direct his men to various strategic positions. With almost drill like precision, the deputies fanned out on either side of us and joined up with two other officers I hadn't seen earlier, but had apparently been at their post watching the back of the cabin. Within less than a minute they had quickly and efficiently surrounded the entire structure. Once this was accomplished we started carefully advancing using whatever cover we could find, the piles of dead pine needles beneath our feet dampening each step. During the several minutes that passed, the area had remained strangely quiet, but as we neared the front porch the air was unexpectedly shattered by the squawking of a nearby jay that stopped us dead in our tracks. We waited an infinitely long minute before continuing, but eventually we took up positions on either side of the entrance. Our weapons still drawn, Bradshaw signaled me to stand ready and with his left hand reached over carefully and rapped on the door.

"Police!" he shouted plainly, so there was no mistaking our identity. "Throw down your weapon and come out with your hands up!"

Another moment passed and then we could distinctly hear movement coming from inside.

"It was an accident!" returned a female voice from behind the door. She sounded extremely nervous. "I was just trying to see if it was loaded and it went off."

"We understand," Bradshaw replied firmly, "but please come out slowly with your hands in plain view!"

The door inched open and Fran Adams came meekly out to greet us. The sheriff pulled her gently aside and then signaled two officers to search the interior of the cabin. Another full minute passed before they returned signaling all clear. During that time we'd remained quiet; the only sound, the slight whispering of a breeze as it traveled across the lake and whistled through the needles of the overhanging pines. As we waited I glanced over at Adams. Simultaneously our eyes met, her expression registering first recognition and then surprise at my presence.

"What are you doing here, Mr.…Logan, wasn't it ?" I nodded. She'd asked this once we'd stepped inside and taken a seat on a couch near the stone fireplace.

"I think that should be obvious," I answered. " I've come to take you back to Los Angeles for questioning." She started to protest, but I quickly reminded her, "You were ordered not to leave town. You've broken the law. You can come of your own accord, or I can have you arrested. It's your call. Either way you're going back with me."

She shrugged and asked that I give her a few minutes to gather her belongings. We had an officer accompany her as she did so.

I didn't waste any time in getting her into the car and back out onto the highway. I estimated that we had only a couple more hours of light and I wanted to be well on our way before nightfall. It was for this reason that I didn't linger waiting for my backup. He was late and I wasn't about to lose daylight waiting on him.

We'd driven a couple of miles in silence, before she broke the ice.

"I guess I'll catch hell from my dad for blowing a hole in the bedroom wall."

"What were you trying to do?" I responded unsympathetically. "Commit suicide?"

"No, nothing so stupid." She wrinkled her nose, and I suddenly noticed that she was attractive, in a girlish sort of way. "I just thought I might need protection, and was checking out my dad's shotgun."

"Protection from what… or should I say whom?" I asked quickly, taking advantage of the opening.

"The killer," she answered cryptically. When I didn't respond, she added, *"You do believe me?"*

"I might. Then again, you could be bluffing."

"What do you mean by that?" she asked startled. "You don't think that I'm the killer do you!"

Before I could answer, I noticed a sedan pull suddenly out from the side road we'd just passed. It was a gray Plymouth, a fairly new model. Within minutes it started to overtake us, and as I glanced through my side view mirror I could see the driver. He was muffled in a red scarf and the rim of his hat was turned down; but of even more interest, he was bearing a sawn-off shotgun and it was aimed in our direction.

I gripped the wheel tightly with my left hand, while reaching over with my right in an attempt to push the girl's head and shoulders below the level of the dash. "Get down; he's got a gun." I warned. Luckily she was a quick study and I was able to instantly return my attention back to the road. The car had now pulled alongside, and I was staring directly into both barrels. The road at this point wasn't very wide, only two lanes each traveling in opposite directions. He was three quarters into the oncoming lane having pushed us close to the shoulder. There was unfortunately no oncoming traffic at that moment, which gave him plenty of room to maneuver. Nevertheless, I turned my wheel hard to the left smashing into him just behind the right front wheel well. The impact made an awful racket of tearing metal and caused him to lose control momentarily as he swerved across and fully into the oncoming lane. I immediately shifted into high gear and floored the accelerator, but he was back onto me in no time. I repeated the action again, but this time he was able to fire off a shot before I sent him careening into the other lane. The girl screamed just as the windshield in front of me disintegrated into thousands of glass fragments. I glanced down quickly to see if she was

OK. She had her arms folded over her head and, at least from my brief inspection, didn't show any signs of injury. Again he was coming, but this time he had to swerve behind me to avoid an oncoming car, its horn blaring. The brief respite gave me time to remove the .45 from my holster, so by the time he caught up again I was ready. As his barrels came up, I fired across my chest through the open window. I really couldn't get a good aim, because I still had to keep an eye on where we were going. I'm not sure if it hit him, but he did fall back momentarily.

I glanced at the speedometer. I was doing close to seventy and the curves were coming fast. The last turn I could almost swear we took on two wheels. To my right the hillside started to drop away which left me very little space to take action. Again he came alongside, but this time I eased up on the accelerator, shifting down so he ended up to the left and slightly ahead of us. I fired a second time, causing his car to swerve into our lane and directly into our path. It happened so quickly that I was not able to break soon enough to avoid smashing into the car's rear. The resulting jolt sent my gun flying across the cabin and out of my reach. He recovered control quickly and pulling forward, switched to the oncoming lane where he started slowing, falling alongside us once again. I didn't see the gun this time. Perhaps he had also lost it in the impact. But instead, he started ramming the front of our car in an attempt to force us off the road. At one point we hit the shoulder kicking up dirt in our path and when I could see clearly again, I realized that he had now forced us closer to the edge of the slope. It didn't leave me many options, and I was quickly calculating them all when something unexpected happened.

Another car, a black Buick roadster, had evidently come up behind and rear ended him, and then passing fast to the left, fired off a shot directly into his vehicle's interior. As I braked to a stop, I simultaneously saw his car fall back and then swerve madly, jumping the edge of the road and bouncing down the steep slope; while looking to my left, I caught a quick glimpse of a red scarf accompanied by a broadly grinning face as the driver of the other car raced past and continued down the road.

I located my gun where it had slid under the dash and then shouting my instructions for her to remain in the car, headed down the road to the point where the car had disappeared over the edge. About fifty feet down the slope the wreckage sat, twisted metal bent like an accordion's bellow crammed between two tree trunks. I started toward it, being careful not to slip on the loose gravel as I made my way down the hillside. As I got nearer I could hear the ping of cooling hot metal and saw a wisp of white steam as water escaped from a crack in the radiator.

Cautiously, I approached the driver's side and peered in. It was empty. Instantly I sensed danger, but even that wasn't enough for me to react in time. In the fraction of a second that I heard behind me the faint sound of a foot upon dry grass, he was upon me. Gripping my gun arm and spinning me around, I came face to face with the killer. Don Taylor! Like a Phoenix rising from the ashes or Lazarus from his tomb, here he stood facing me. He was pretty beat up from the accident, but obviously still fit enough to take me on. Maybe he was just filled with adrenaline. He was certainly growling like a mad man when I faced him, as saliva mixed with blood was drooling down his chin. The hat was now gone, but the scarf was still hanging loosely around his neck.

He slammed my right arm against the car door, causing me to lose the grip on my automatic. As it hit the ground he kicked it further, causing it to slide beneath the car and subsequently out of sight. He hadn't his shotgun, and I was to learn later why. It became wedged between the passenger seat and floor during the crash. Pinning me with his left arm, he removed the scarf with his right and brought it up menacingly to my neck. It was no mystery what his intentions were as I stared into his insane eyes. There was also no question that I was not going to sit still for it; and so in answer, I brought my knee up with all the force I could into his mid-section. He staggered back with the impact and I closely followed it with a right upper cut to the side of his cheek. Doubled over, he charged me like a bull, catching me full in the chest and knocking me back against the side of the car. He then recovered nicely, firing off two punches in rapid succession; one blow to my stomach and the other to my chin. I was starting to hurt, but I was also getting mad. He swung again with his fist, but I was ready for him blocking it with my arm. He then tried swinging at me with his left and again I blocked. As he stepped back to reappraise the situation, I saw an opening and took it. He had stumbled slightly, perhaps due to a loose rock, but it diverted his attention away from me long enough that I was able to successfully launch both a right and a left to the side of his head, and then a solid punch to his solar plexus. As he doubled over I delivered my final powerhouse to his chin, which lifted him off his feet and flat onto his back unconscious.

Exhausted, I dropped to the ground, my legs no longer strong enough to support me. Eventually I dragged myself toward one of the pine trees and rising up on one elbow, came up to a sitting position using its trunk as a support. I was still breathing heavy, my throat was dry, and when I coughed, I spat up some blood. Behind me I heard the sound of gravel cascading down the slope and although I was too tired to turn, I knew it was the girl. I felt like hell, and I think she saw it in my eyes as she came rushing to my side.

"Why do you do it, Logan?" she asked, in apparent concern. She reached up to touch my cheek and I winched from the pain.

"Maybe it's because my mother believed in God and my dad, justice." I tried to laugh, but it hurt too much. Figuring that I owed her a more serious explanation, I added, "Perhaps I'm not as cynical as I look. Maybe I believe the world is worth saving. Mankind might be apathetic, but I still sense a lot of good in them. Sure they may be waiting for some other guy to stand up in their place...they being too weak to go it alone. Well, let's just say I'm that other guy...saving the world from itself...if only one bit at a time."

I don't know what brought that to the surface. Perhaps it was just the weariness of the case. However she must have liked what I said, because she smiled, gently adding,

"Well, you certainly are my Saint George!"

I felt more like Don Quixote, and I didn't have the heart to tell her that this wasn't over. There was still one more dragon to slay.

20

TYING LOOSE ENDS

It's one thing to gather the information; it's another to piece it all together so it makes sense. These murders have been like one giant puzzle. You have all the parts, but they are upside down, or twisted, and it takes a great deal of concentration and tons of patience before you get them to fit exactly into place.

"Logan!" I heard a voice shout from behind. "Do you need help?"

Well that question wouldn't win any prizes for brilliance. I raised a painful eyebrow at Adams and then turned to see who this Einstein was. It was Hansen from Homicide. My backup.

Perhaps I was being too hard on him, he was young, but in the past I've found that sarcasm and my pain level usually ran neck and neck with each other, and that was probably why I was being so critical of him. I wanted to say that I could've used his help about five minutes earlier, but opted instead for, "could you come down here and cuff him?"

He nodded and made his way down the slope. Adams took me by the arm and aided me back up to the road. As we reached the top, a couple of sheriff's cars came screeching to a halt and Bradshaw jumped out.

"We received a report of gunshots."

I outlined briefly what had happened and then asked that he contact their San Bernardino office and put out an A.P.B. for a black Buick roadster, California plates, license number unknown.

"The car should stand out because of damage to the front end," I added. "The driver's name is Rappo, Victorio Aldo Rappo. He should be held and booked on attempted murder."

The rest of the arrangements fortunately proved less eventful. I commandeered Hansen's vehicle. I needed it to get the girl back to LA. I didn't trust the automobile I had been driving. It was pretty banged up, and ended up having to be towed to a local garage. I carefully thought through the situation and decided that it might be risky to move Adams and the prisoner in the same vehicle. Therefore, Hansen was to stay behind with the prisoner in San Bernardino. Here Taylor would be contained in a holding cell until Red could send a car to transport them both back to Los Angeles.

It was getting late by the time we finally hit the road. For the early part of the trip Adams was quiet, almost brooding. But as time wore on I could sense a growing anger in her which finally reached a point where she seemed anxious to talk. I wasn't going to discourage her.

"I can't believe Taylor tried to kill me!" she blurted out. "I just can't understand it!"

"What's not to understand?" I responded calmly. "He felt you were a threat. Perhaps he was afraid you would finger him."

"Finger him for what?"

"Murder."

"That's ridiculous."

"It's the only explanation that makes sense." I was going to say more, but something told me not to… at least not for the moment. I took another route.

"Then why were you hiding?"

"I wasn't hiding!" she replied emphatically.

"You disappeared pretty quickly after the murder, and you didn't leave word with anyone…including your colleagues at work. It sounds to me like you were running from something." I then added quickly, "Guilt, perhaps?"

She shook her head vehemently. "I have nothing to be guilty of!"

"Then you were hiding from your blackmailer?"

"How'd you know I was being blackmailed?" she responded sharply.

"By the same way I know that you're pregnant."

This caught her totally by surprise, and she sat dumbfounded for some seconds before attempting to respond. And when she did it was unintelligible. Just a series of mumbles.

I pressed further. "That's what he's got on you, isn't it?"

She just stared at me again with her mouth open, so I decided to throw another idea at her, "Can you say for certain that Taylor isn't the guy putting the 'touch' on you?"

It was a shot in the dark, stated in an attempt to bring her back to reality. It accomplished that in spades, and in the process elicited an interesting response.

"Don Taylor- a blackmailer? No. That's impossible, he's…" she stammered for a second, as if catching herself, and then grew strangely quiet.

After a pause I asked, "He's what?"

"He couldn't have possibly known," she replied firmly.

"But you were being blackmailed," I pressed again. "Isn't that why you put the drug in Geary's cup?"

Again I caught her by surprise. She thought for a long moment and then replied, "Yes. I was told that my pregnancy would be made known if I didn't cooperate. But it wasn't Don Taylor…" Here she seemed at odds with herself. "I mean…. I was left a note that was all. It said that Soames would give me a drug that I was to place in her cup. It specifically stated that it wasn't poison, just something to make her uncomfortable."

So by her account, my conjecture earlier about Soames was correct. Another thought struck me. If this was all pre-planned, someone had to be sure that Geary would have something to spike.

"Who suggested that Geary get some coffee?"

"That was also part of the instructions." Adams now seemed embarrassed. "Originally at a pre-arranged time I was supposed to bring her the cup. She just made it easy for me by getting it herself. All I had to do was slip the drug in when she wasn't looking."

I remembered that Geary had found it necessary to contact Rappo and used the trip to Craft Services as an excuse.

"And what time was this pre-arranged moment?" I asked.

"About 10:00 a.m."

That would figure. I was expected to arrive by ten, and calculating any delays, or being temporarily held up at the gate, and then allowing for the ten minute walk to the set, it would take anywhere from fifteen to thirty minutes for me to arrive at the scene. As I recall *Chloral Hydrate* takes about that long to take effect.

"There was also something else," she began hesitatingly, as she seemed to be carefully weighing her next words. "Earlier that morning I saw something. It didn't seem important at the time, but its significance hit me later… actually much later. I had forgotten all about it until I reached Arrowhead, but I saw Mattie placing a glass of water under the workbench in the property area."

A long pause followed. I was still absorbing this disturbing revelation of hers, when she suddenly switched topics and asked coyly, "Earlier you said you suspected that I might be the killer. Why?"

"Oh, I don't know. Maybe it's because you ran… or maybe it was that incident back at the cabin. It seems you're not afraid of firearms."

She laughed. "You got to be kidding! I nearly shot off my foot with my daddy's shotgun. What makes you think I would be any better with a revolver?"

It wasn't the response I had expected from the girl, and for a brief moment it quite honestly confused me. However, after a pause I decided to move on, reminded of another important question I'd meant to ask of her. "You were part of that exclusive group that hung around Geary that day… why do you think Betty Jean Williams was killed? What had she seen, or heard?"

Again she seemed indecisive… or perhaps she was just reasoning it out. In any case, after a pause she said resignedly, "She had gone over to Clemmons to report that Geary wasn't feeling well. He told her to sit Geary down and have Hyland get some water. When she got back, and before she could say anything, Hyland issued the same orders… *almost word for word.* Betty Jean confided in me that it seemed strange the two of them using those exact words. Almost as if the incident was orchestrated. In fact, I believe that was how she put it… that it 'all seemed orchestrated.'"

We had gotten in late the previous night, or perhaps it was early that next morning. In any case, I was pretty tired the following day as I got an early start, reporting to Red at his office. I was pretty beat up, and it seemed like anything that moved hurt. There were a few bruises on my body and a cut on my cheek that I bandaged. I knew Red would have some comment when I walked in, and of course he didn't disappoint.

"Did ya git da license of da truck dat hit ya?"

"No," I replied wearily, "but Taylor will soon be making them!"

I was referring to a prison metal shop where the inmates banged out auto licenses. It was a pretty picture that I had formed in my head of Taylor spending countless hours laboring there.

"How's Miss Adams?" Red asked, in concern. "Hope she fared better than yar self."

"She's OK," I answered, and then added thoughtfully, "better keep an eye on her however. Could you send a matron over to her house?"

Just as he was agreeing to my request, a telephone rang and he was called away by the officer who had answered it. Red spoke briefly with whoever was on the other end, and then returned with the news that Rappo had been picked up by the sheriff 's department; apparently late that previous night, and stranded on the highway. They would be sending him down to Los Angeles within the hour.

Good. I had some further questions I needed to ask of him, and his presence would add to the gathering I had in mind for later.

"What's the status on that inquiry with Vice?" I asked. "Were they able to get any information out of the two they picked up?"

"One of them played canary," Red replied with a smile. "He said that he'd supplied Soames with a small bottle of *Chloral Hydrate* two days before da murder."

"Good," I said. "That seems to be the final word we need regarding that aspect of the investigation. Adams admitted receiving it from Soames and this information confirms it."

I spent a good part of that day and most of the next following leads and tying up loose ends. I had a good idea of how it all fit together, and whatever way you looked at it, the outcome was not pretty. I must have made a dozen phone calls and looked over a ton of notes, prison reports, court transcripts, and police interviews. Red's men had done an excellent job questioning Gioani and had made a typewritten account available to me so I could fill in some enormous holes which related to background. I factored them into my account. I also asked additional questions by phone of just about everyone involved in the investigation. That is, of those who were still breathing. Clemmons and I went over some old ground and then discussed the more personal aspects of his health. He also cleared the path so I could confirm what he'd told me with his physician. I talked with Mr. Hyland and likewise got similar information regarding his daughter, and finally I contacted the Santa Barbara Education Department in regards to Adams' school records, and did a quick background check on Taylor with some contacts I had back east. Some of this information, I'll admit, was circumstantial, but others had a direct bearing on the case. However, if I was to present a thorough explanation of the events leading up to, and after the murders, it was essential that I get *all* the facts and make damn sure that they lined up like pretty little ducks in a row!

When I felt I had put it together as well as I could, I asked Red to do two things. I needed him to get a search warrant and send some men to check over one of the suspect's former lodgings, and then to arrange with Jack Clemmons that we have the use of his home for the following night. I thought it was time to end this drama, and I wanted all the players, including Taylor, gathered on stage for the final act!

Clemmons was sub-leasing an unusual home located in the Hollywood Hills. Its architect, Frank Lloyd Wright, was exceptionally creative in his designs, and this was no exception. The house was constructed of concrete blocks in a modular pattern with repeating mosaic designs. The doors and windows were made up of art glass, which varied in intensity from dark to light as you looked from top to bottom. However, one of the most striking features and arguably the most unusual yet intriguing was the metal work, whose designs were copied directly from Mayan artwork. It gave the place a mysterious, foreboding character, like some grandiose sacrificial temple, which in a sense was what the place had come to represent since that now infamous night that Clemmons held his Hollywood party. It was for this reason that I selected it for this evening's gathering, where unfortunately one final sacrifice would have to be made.

An assortment of automobiles passed through the large iron gate at 7:00 p.m. and found areas to park in the courtyard. Red made sure that there were plenty of police present around the mansion; some obvious and some not. These men were especially vigilant when the police wagon pulled up and both Taylor and Rappo, shackled with handcuffs, were escorted inside. We all gathered in the main living room, a large space flanked by numerous square columns trimmed with Mayan designs. The centerpiece of this open area was a stone fireplace, beautifully accented by a wisteria motif of intricate mosaics that were inlaid directly above the mantle. The two ladies, Hyland and Adams, were dressed for cocktails, Rappo was in his usual attire complete with scarf, Taylor was already in prison garb, and Clemmons was dressed as if for tennis. It was an odd assembly, but then again, this *was* Hollywood.

I waited until everyone had assembled before speaking. Each found themselves a convenient chair or place on one of two comfortable leather couches to settle into. It was a mild night; twinkling lights from the L.A. basin could be viewed through an enormous window which ran from floor to ceiling. However, the house itself was cold, even colder than the stare I was getting from Taylor. Clemmons, playing the good host, built a hot, crackling fire. It was toward this fireplace that the assembly was now facing, and the location that I chose to begin delivering my summations. I stalled for a few minutes in the beginning hoping that Red's men would return from their search with the one final, although not totally necessary, piece to the puzzle. Clemmons used this delay to ask if he should serve drinks.

"I'd rather not," I replied at his request, "for two very good reasons. One, you'd be breaking the law. Think about it, the place is packed with cops…"

"I'm sure if we grease a few palms they'll turn the other way," he offered.

"I'll pretend I didn't hear that," I replied sternly. "I once busted a guy's jaw for suggesting something similar!"

"You really are a boy scout, Logan," he remarked grudgingly. "What's the other reason?"

"I'll need clear minds. The tale I'm about to spin is long and complex… even for the sharpest of intellects, and I don't need booze clouding them up."

By 7:45 I noticed some officers enter the room and make directly for Red. They spoke with him for a moment, and I saw them indicate a parcel under their arm. He sent them away with the package, but not before consulting with me as to their findings. So now finally, I was ready to begin, and the curtain could go up on the first act!

21

THE CURTAIN RISES ON ACT 1

Now it was time to take center stage, and under the spotlight deliver my monologue. Fortunately, I didn't have opening night jitters, confident in the fact that I held a captive audience. At least two of them were already in handcuffs.

As I stood up I glanced at all the faces of the group gathered around me. Some looked bored, others looked angry or anxious, and there was even a sprinkling of those who seemed amused at having been summoned there that evening. But they all became focused on me when I began to speak. "I know I don't have to introduce myself, or give you an explanation of why you were called here this evening. You know me, and you know why you are here. Three brutal murders and a couple of attempts have occurred during the last two weeks… one just a couple of days ago. Now, all of these are connected together, but the strands leading to them are complex and have taken many different turns.

"To begin with, I have chosen this house as a setting for this denouncement with a purpose, for in some ways it was here that it all began, at a party that was held about eight months ago. However, to really grasp the entire story we will need to go back even further… perhaps a year or two…"

I walked over to where Rappo was sitting and pointed him out to the crowd. "This is Victorio Aldo Rappo. I'm sure many of you recognize him as the man hanging around the studio during the week of the murder, and the man Soames noted as having fled the scene just after the killing. It was most readily pointed out at the time by Taylor that this man had connections with the mob. One of the few statements made by him that, I may add, was the truth." I looked at Taylor, but he was staring down at his feet. "Rappo worked back east as an enforcer for 'Joe the Boss' Masseria, but was ousted by one 'Lucky Luciano' when he came out to the west coast on a supposed mission to stake out new territory for the mob. Here Rappo hooked up with a Bugsy Segal want-to-be, a minor crook named Gioani who was running some petty scam operations for chump change. Ready to graduate up, Gioani convinced Rappo to form an alliance, and they set about creating an organization that would deal in blackmail." I looked down at Rappo and I could see that he looked surprised. I went on to explain, "I was able to get this from the horse's mouth. We had some men interview Gioani and this, and what is to follow, comes pretty much from his own words. But let's continue. Both Gioani and Rappo figured L.A. was the perfect location for blackmail… after all, its industry was ripe with scandal… and all they really needed was a means to gain access to the inside and its dirty little secrets. Here they decided to set up a machine which would call for the enlistment of certain people already in the motion picture business. Their first discovery was an out of work actress named Geary. Her real name was O'Malley, but more on that later. She came to L.A. with hopes of stardom, but was damn near skid row when they'd discovered her. She was young, beautiful, and more importantly, willing to do anything to survive. They used her at first as bait for the old Badger routine, but ultimately their plan was to focus her talents on gathering information from inside the studio. Here gossip could be overheard and things could be observed, and Geary was a keen observer."

Again I purposely looked at Rappo. "Remember she told you something didn't feel right just before she was murdered? I think that gives you an idea of just how keen her observations were." He nodded weakly. I continued, "But in order for that scheme to work, she had to get employment and up to that time she had not been successful, hence the need of our fourth character, Don Taylor. Taylor was a working assistant director, but carrying some heavy debts... most of them due to illegal gambling. Rappo discovered him through a conversation he had with Lou 'The Dice' Dutch who ran the gambling establishment Taylor frequented. Dutch had told him that Taylor's losses had gotten so bad that he had ordered his boys to apply 'pressure.' He was then instructed to pay up by the end of the month or accept the consequences. What exactly those consequences were was anybody's guess, but Taylor knew it couldn't be good. However, for Rappo the timing couldn't have been any better, and using this knowledge he enticed Taylor to join his team. His offer was to take care of the debt, and even to 'sweeten the deal' by promising a fairly generous 'cut' if his contributions started bearing fruit. His main job was simply to make sure that Geary received employment, and perhaps offer a little information if it happened to come his way.

"Initially the set up worked pretty well, they had either gathered the information on individuals who were not discreet in their activities, or when that dried up they created 'traps' for unwary victims to fall into. The real payoff came, however, when Miss Hyland was employed by the studio about... ten months ago?" I looked toward her for confirmation, and she nodded her head. "You might say that this was the beginning of another thread that led ultimately to the murders. For to this gang she represented the Mother Lode or

El Dorado. Here was the heiress to the Hyland Milk fortune, a victim that can be, excuse the pun, milked for hundreds of thousands. Now, the girl herself didn't have any vices, unless naivety is counted, which it's not. So they had to set her up. Clemmons house party became the trap and some liquor, drugs, and a handy photographer did the rest." I looked over at Hyland. I could tell that she wasn't enjoying this part of the tale, and I would've spared her of it, but it was an essential thread. The best I could do was not dwell on it too long. I continued again after a short pause. "Well, the dividends started paying off immediately, and that's when the greed set in. Taylor was a charmer. He had Geary eating out of his hand. He was tall, handsome, and endearing in many of his ways. She was attracted to him, and shortly started believing that there was something between them. He, in turn, did little to suggest otherwise… in fact he encouraged it, because it would ultimately ensure his plans."

I stopped here to see if I still had their attention. I had. Picking up from where I left off, I continued, "Gioani, as I mentioned, was nothing until Rappo came along. And Taylor used every opportunity to remind Rappo of it… even suggesting that Rappo would do better if he ran the outfit totally on his own. Taylor even went so far as to suggest that Rappo was really the brains, and Gioani was just sitting back collecting on the goods. Eventually it worked. The seeds of discord had taken root, and they both settled on a plan to

squeeze Gioani out. Geary was also in, totally mesmer-
ized by Taylor's boyish charms and winning ways. So,
now, the next thread. Me.

"I was approached by Taylor to help him out of
a jam he'd gotten into… or so he said. He came to
my office about six months ago with a story that he'd
become a 'mark' in a Badger scheme. He was photo-
graphed in a compromising position with a woman,
and seeing that he was in the midst of a messy divorce,
he needed my help. Something didn't seem right with
the guy from the moment I met him. Perhaps it was just
my gift of discernment working overtime, but since I
couldn't exactly put my finger on it, I accepted his case.
Stated simply, Gioani was set up and they used me as
the dupe to nail him. Rappo himself had stayed clear
of the scheme by agreement; passive resistance. They
felt that he was too connected with organized crime to
escape the fallout that was sure to follow. Therefore,
by arrangement, he took off while Geary and Taylor
set the wheels in motion. Geary, by the way, was a professional name she'd adopted after this period. Her
real name was Bridget O'Malley and that was what she
was using at the time I became aware of her. She had
looked slightly different then, and there was enough of
a change that I didn't readily recognize her when I saw
her briefly at the studio…" I then added quickly, "And
besides, she was lying face down, and the shock of the
moment can dull even my perception."

Again I stopped and looked around. I still had their rapt attention. Good. I continued.

"So Taylor played the victim, Geary the bait, and they both made sure that my investigation led to Gioani. It all seemed too easy. Taylor made it clear from the beginning that the girl was to be exonerated if possible. His excuse being that he wasn't as concerned with her actions as he was with the person who put her up to it. And I believe it was Taylor's idea to suggest to his lawyer to make a deal with the D.A's office to get her off if she cooperated with the investigation. Of course there was never any question that she would. It was the plan all along. In the end Gioani ended up at San Quentin, Geary received a slap on the wrist receiving only probation, and Rappo returned home to take over the gang... leaving now only three 'cuts' to make instead of four, and they would all become richer for it." I walked back over to where Rappo was seated. As he looked up I gestured toward him saying, "Up to this point I was relating the story as told to me by Gioani; now this next part is courtesy of Mr. Rappo here." I caught an exchange of glares between Taylor and Rappo. "Starting about three months ago, Taylor's attitude started changing. He seemed to be taking on the decision making for the team's operation against Rappo's wishes. A rift formed between them, and Rappo saw the signs that he might be squeezed out again like he was by Luciano. Taylor was manipulative;

he realized that now. After all, he had managed it with Gioani.

"Now, the reasons for Taylor's move at this point I'll admit are conjecture, but based on facts as I know them." I looked at Taylor. "Of course he's welcome to correct me if I'm wrong." I think he growled and mumbled something. Ignoring him, I continued, "About this time he started cozying up to our next thread, Fran Adams, while also making in-roads with Hyland. Neither knew of the other, which says something about his ability to successfully juggle, but he was able to pull it off. That is until Adams became pregnant…"

"I don't think we need to…" Adams began suddenly, as she rose from her chair.

"I'm sorry, but I think we do," I replied, interrupting her. "It too, has a bearing on the case…" I felt like a cad, but I wasn't hired to be nice, only to get results. "Especially *since Taylor is the father!*" A gasp arose from the crowd, and a second protest arose from Adams.

"You don't know that, Logan!"

"Well, I wasn't there, if that's what you mean, but you just about told me on our trip back from Arrowhead. It got me thinking, and when I returned I called your old boyfriend. It escaped me when he'd spoken at the time… maybe it was because I was so focused on Clemmons for reasons I will state shortly, but when I asked him who he suspected you were seeing at the studio, he said 'one of the directors' on the picture you were working on, not 'The Director.' Taylor is an 'Assistant Director.' I just assumed it was Clemmons."

I looked over at Taylor. He grinned, but it didn't extend to his eyes, as he answered with a shrug: "What difference does it make. Sure. It's my kid."

"Of course you didn't want that known then," I said, returning to my narrative. "In fact you circulated the rumor that it was Clemmons', because you'd learned from her that she'd been having an occasional affair with Clemmons ever since that night of the party, thereby turning this unwelcomed revelation of hers into a useful tool of blackmail against him."

Taylor clapped his hands mockingly, and then asked, "What made you so sure that it wasn't Clemmons' kid after all?"

"With his permission I had a talk with his doctor yesterday. I'll spare you the details, but he's incapable of having children. He and his wife have been trying for years. He only allowed himself to be blackmailed because sometimes the accusation can do more harm than the truth... and besides there was still the question of his wife, the affair, and what public exposure would do to their relationship."

I took a deep breath and made a sweep of the room. I could tell that some of the eyes were starting to glaze over, so I apologized.

"I know that I may seem a little longwinded, but I told you from the start that the route to the solution of this case was complex and I must ask for your further indulgence." I paused to gather my thoughts, and then continued, "Now, while this is going on, his charms are starting to work on Miss Hyland. And here again I am going to venture out and say that this power over her may have been the impetus for his change from a submissive to a leadership role in the gang. But for whatever reason, it was becoming more and more apparent to both Rappo and Geary that Taylor was going to make some move which would cut them both out of the operation, and the sweet payoff that they were receiving at Hyland's expense." I suddenly remembered something I needed to add. "Geary, as you remember, had early designs on Taylor. It couldn't have been sitting too well with her when she saw both Adams and Hyland now in the picture, and she being forced to take a back seat. They say nothing is fiercer than the wrath of a spurned woman. Well according to Rappo, that was the case. It was her idea to beat Taylor to the punch. She and Rappo started removing the various pieces of evidence they had collected on their victims, and created their own records… a black book… or journal with all the information they needed to strike out on their own. When that was all accomplished about a month ago, they gave Taylor the boot."

I paused again, only this time it was calculated for dramatic effect. After all this was the capital of entertainment. The spotlight was on me and I was now ready to introduce act two.

"We now come to the point of my story where things really start getting ugly, and two women are killed for the oldest of motivations—GREED."

22

ACT TWO: THE DRAMA UNFOLDS

Perhaps my little speech was coming over a tad melodramatic. But in truth, there's nothing more tragic than senseless murder, and so I couldn't explain it any other way.

" **W**hat Taylor had initially planned is anybody's guess, however what ultimately made him decide to take the actions he did was undoubtedly due to the fact that he'd been threatened by his former colleagues. They demanded that he go quiet or risk exposure. So, in point of fact, he himself was now the victim of his own blackmail scheme. Immediately, I believe, he started searching for a way out, and it was then that he settled on what he thought was the perfect plan. It was similar to what had worked before, but somewhat more refined and definitely *more* complicated. It would take the co-operation of Miss Hyland, but she was already under his spell. In essence his plan would begin by revealing the fact that both Rappo and Geary were her black-mailers, which was the truth. He just conveniently left himself out… and then convinced her that the only safe and permanent solution to her problem was a plan he'd come up with himself… one that involved murder. What else he promised to get her to play along, I can't honestly say… unless either of you would be willing to volunteer this information?" I looked at both Taylor and Hyland, who did their best to ignore me. When I didn't elicit a response, I continued, "I thought not. But, let's say for instance, that he argued that going to the police with this information still risked her secret going public, and that the best solution was to handle it his way. Well, whatever ruse he used worked; she signed onto his plan and he set the wheels into motion.

"Now, Taylor, like all of you, is in the film business. He understands taking a thought, committing it to a script, and bringing it to life. Of course what's pro-duced for a film is only fantasy projected onto a screen for the pleasure of a movie audience. Well, this script of his wasn't being designed for entertainment. This was for real. There wouldn't be actors playing dead up on the screen, but actual victims who would be stone cold as the result of his plotting."

Again Taylor interrupted, clapping his hands in a mocking manner, while stating arrogantly, "Very pretty little speech, but a tad over dramatic wouldn't you say, Logan?" Perhaps he had a point. But I wasn't going to let him get my goat. I ignored him and continued.

"First stage in his plan was to get his victims close to him. That was easy. It was as simple as hiring Geary on as a bit actress for that week. He knew that they would be suspicious, and all the better because that meant that she would drag Rappo along for the bargain. He counted on it, and would use his presence for reasons I will explain later.

"The second was to establish that Hyland was being threatened from someone inside the studio. The note they made up from the letters cut from the script would establish that fact, but because these were so tightly controlled they needed to cut up one other than their own. Hence Clemmons' was acquired. Taylor just used the blackmail routine, substituting a monetary payoff for the script instead. Clemmons thought it odd, but just figured that it had some value to the blackmailer, that perhaps he had a buyer. In any case, he had no idea what it was really being used for until I dropped that information in his lap during our lunch together last week.

"Next he needed a dupe to act as a witness. Here I enter again. I'd worked well for him the first time, and so he figured I'd probably serve just as useful for this caper. He had Hyland come to my office with the bogus note and the story they cooked up to lure me to the studio the next day. She had set up the time, so they knew within five or ten minutes when I should arrive. Now, I should also mention at this point that a few arrangements had been made to set the stage. Their chosen victim was Geary, and the illusion had to be made that she was mistakenly killed instead of Hyland. As far as age, weight, height, and hair color was concerned they were similar, however Hyland had worn her hair long, while Geary's was short. Of course the solution was easy… just have it cut and styled like their intended victim. When I visited Hyland's home the other day, I noticed a photo of her with her hair done up for a social function. It was long. Her father informed me that it was taken just a day or so before she came to my office where it was definitely cut the same as Geary's. I found that terribly suggestive. The next sleight of hand came in what they were wearing. Taylor knew that Geary would be dressed in the white… or off-white uniform of a nurse, so Hyland made sure that the blouse she wore that day was similar in design and coloring.

"Incidentally, Hyland wasn't the only one masquerading. Taylor adopted the unique costume of Rappo for my benefit during Hyland's visit to my office. She had made a point at that meeting of mentioning she was being followed. Naturally I would be on the lookout when she asked me to walk her out of my building and see her into a cab. Taylor also wore the disguise on a few other occasions, always with the aim of directing the suspicion back onto Rappo. Taylor knew with a certainty, and calculated it into his plan, that Rappo would flee the scene of the murder; either out of self-preservation, for fear of being killed himself by a second shot coming from the unknown assassin, or from the police who would regard him with suspicion because of his mob connections. This was how he planned to rid himself of Rappo. Keep him on the run…and if that didn't work he figured he could always find some way later to discreetly dispose of him when things quieted down.

"But returning to Geary, Taylor reasoned that it would also bolster their deception if, when murdered, she was found in the script supervisor's chair…the chair assigned to Hyland. This, however, would not be as easy to accomplish as the others, but could be arranged with a little engineering. It required getting two other people involved in the plot, which under normal circumstances would seem somewhat risky, but as I will explain later, wasn't as chancy as it seemed. The first person needed was Soames. He was to supply a drug. Taylor most likely applied the same tactics of blackmail to him as he did with Clemmons to acquire this item. Soames passed it, as instructed, to Adams, who placed it into Geary's coffee cup when she wasn't looking. The object of the drug was to cause dizziness and create a need for Geary to be seated in the script supervisor's chair when offered by Hyland. Timing was important here, and as Adams told me on our trip back from Arrowhead, she was instructed to place it in the cup at a specific time that was calculated so the drug would take effect close to the moment of my arrival. Again it was tricky, but it worked. The induced illness also had another function, actually more important than the first. It gave the killer an excuse to leave the scene, and prepare for the kill in an area specifically set up for it. That location was the property area, and Taylor made sure in his function as assistant director that everyone, including Soames, would steer clear of there just prior to the murder. Taylor was probably the one who had suggested to Clemmons that the 'extras' were not holding their weapons properly and that the prop man was to watch the action from the sound booth area. Now, the property area was perfect for their needs; it had several boxes to hide behind, weapons left on a work bench, any of which could be used lethally with the substitution of a real bullet, and it was situated off to one side of the set and somewhat isolated. I'm not sure how much of this Taylor actually arranged, although I imagine that in his capacity as assistant director the placement of various pieces of equipment on the set could come under his supervision. One thing was certain, however; the day, time, and location of the murder was selected by him to maximize their advantage. All the chaos on the battle set, and the noise, including gunshots, gave them the perfect cover… and I'm sure the chairs themselves were also positioned by him to allow a perfect line of sight for the killer."

I noticed Hyland start to squirm, and I gave Red the eye to move a man nearer to her position. Once

I saw him in place, I continued again. "When Geary said she felt ill, Miss Hyland suggested that she be seated, and then offered to get her a glass of water. She never went to Craft Services, however, because the glass had already been collected earlier and was waiting for her, concealed under a bench in the property area. She herself had placed it there to buy some time and thus account for the total length of her absence." At this point Hyland started to jump up in protest, but a hand on her shoulder by the officer sat her firmly back down. "I know this because Adams told me that she had stumbled on her hiding the glass earlier that morning. Hyland didn't see her, and Adams instantly dismissed it, not recalling it until later when she had reached Arrowhead.

"So, having the previous perimeters in place, all that was left for the execution of the plan was to get Hyland in position at the prop area and wait for my grand entrance. A gun was placed in a special location at the end of the bench, where she was told that it would be loaded with live ammunition. Again timing was important, but luck and knowledge of my reliability worked in their favor. The shot was fired the moment I appeared on the scene and the murder committed under my very eyes exactly as Taylor planned it."

At that moment Hyland unexpectedly swooned and all eyes turned toward her. A police matron rushed to her side and worked quickly at reviving her.

"So it was Hyland who killed Geary?" Clemmons stated, shaking his head in disbelief.

"No," I corrected him. "You were not following exactly what I was saying."

I waited until they revived her before continuing. She asked to be excused, but I declined her request with the explanation that it would be to her benefit to stay. I know I probably seemed like the big bad wolf, but after all this wasn't a Sunday social *and we were discussing murder.*

When things settled down, I began again. "What I just related was what was *supposed* to have happened and, in part, some of it had. However even with the simplest and most carefully laid plans there is always a possibility for error... and this plan was neither simple, nor as carefully thought out as Taylor's ego had convinced him. For one thing, he didn't anticipate Rappo's reactions correctly. He did run, but not too far. He wasn't afraid of Taylor or even the chance that his involvement in the blackmail schemes would be discovered. Although, I may add, he did what he could to cover them. No, his real concern was to clear himself of the murders and in the process get back at Taylor. That was why he went to Betty Jean's apartment that night presumably to find the book, and then showed up a day later at my office. And in turn, after that tussle they had at the apartment, Taylor realized that Rappo wasn't going to be as easy a problem to solve as he'd originally planned, and so kept a careful eye on him, as in the instance when he tailed him to my office. If it wasn't for a certain 'item' that they were both interested in… Taylor would have tried killing him, and Rappo undoubtedly would have done the same. Of course not knowing exactly how much Rappo had told me, Taylor still carried on the masquerade as Rappo right up to the end… maybe not so much to convince me, but to confuse other witnesses. He was dressed like him when he did that little performance with the shotgun at the Hyland mansion, and again when Adams and I were attacked on the way back from Arrowhead."

"What 'item' was that?" Clemmons suddenly asked, interrupting my narrative.

"In answer to that we need to introduce our next thread, Betty Jean Williams, and how she also became an unexpected and unwelcomed player in Taylor's plan. As you know, she was Geary's roommate and, as it turns out, trusted friend. I don't believe that she had known exactly what Geary was into, although, in truth, it doesn't really make any difference to the chain of events if she did. When their apartment was broken into by Taylor… and I believe it's safe to say that it was him looking for the 'item' I just mentioned, a journal … a book filled with dirty little secrets on just about everyone in this room, it scared Geary enough that she asked Betty Jean to take the book and hide it. No doubt reasoning that whatever her friend came up with would be more secure than any she could find. And she did, the action ultimately costing her, her life. Although, sadly, I, too, may be to blame; and the unfortunate coincidence of her being called as an 'extra' that day on the set. Taylor wanted a witness, but not one that would be that close to his victim during the time of the murder..."

"But wait a minute," interrupted Adams. "Why didn't Taylor just have Betty Jean released from the set. He could have as an assistant director?"

"I can answer that," Clemmons volunteered. "Taylor did suggest it to me. I can't remember the reason, but I told him no. She was the only woman 'extra' hired that day and we needed her for the shot. To ask Central Casting at that point to send another would've delayed filming."

"Well, whatever the case," I continued, reclaiming the floor, "she was there, and too close to the action as far as Taylor was concerned. He was afraid she would either see or hear something... *and she did.* According to Adams, Betty Jean reported to Clemmons when Geary became ill and some conversation occurred there that drew her suspicions. Just as an aside, up to this point I don't think Betty Jean was aware at all about Taylor's involvement."

Clemmons started to say something, but I waved him off preferring to listen to Rappo instead.

"Vicki was extremely careful in what she told Betty Jean. She was a good kid... innocent to the world...

and Vicki wanted to keep her that way. Vicki came up with this story that we told her… that Vicki and I were working undercover with the police and had gotten hold of a blackmailer's journal that the mob wanted back. Taylor's name was never mentioned. Nor anyone else's for that matter. Vicki figured the less the girl knew the safer it would be for all of us."

"She may have been innocent, but she wasn't naïve," I added. "I believe she wanted to know exactly what it was that she was protecting. That is why she opened the package when it was in her possession, to actually see what was inside. It told her nothing, however, for it was in code." I paused to remember where I had left off in the narrative. "But getting back to my story; Betty Jean went to Clemmons…"

"But it wasn't me," Clemmons interrupted again. "I told you so at lunch last week."

"And I believe you," I responded. "However this is what Adams told me, but I suspect that she may've been mistaken."

Now it was Adams turn to protest, but I held up a hand to silence her. "Adams said that Betty Jean talked to Clemmons and reported that Geary was ill. However, as you will see in a moment, the person I believe Betty Jean had most likely reported to was Taylor. I'll continue to explain it in that way. Taylor had told her to sit Geary down and have Hyland fetch some water. When she returned to the women, Hyland repeating those same orders almost verbatim. It was odd, and she remarked as such to Adams. Of course aside from the coincidence, it didn't seem all that important, until the murder occurred. After that, it took on more significance. It was that which Betty Jean was referring to when she approached me at the studio. Unfortunately she spotted Taylor over my shoulder, and when I asked who had issued the orders, she lied and said Clemmons. She said it loud enough, I'm sure, for Taylor's benefit, but the fact that she lied undoubtedly erased any doubts that he had about her not suspecting him. That she didn't tell the truth indicated that she was afraid of him… and quite incidentally it was this reaction of Betty Jean's that makes me accept Clemmons' explanation over Adams'. I also feel that the accusation leveled at Rappo by the crew was something else she had wanted to mention to me. As Rappo just said, she knew him as Geary's ally. According to their story, an undercover agent, so there was no way that he could have been the murderer."

"I'd like to add something," Rappo interrupted again. I nodded, and he continued, "You mentioned earlier that I went to Betty Jean's apartment to retrieve the journal. That was only partially the reason. I was also afraid that Taylor would do something stupid to Betty Jean. I knew Vicki slipped and told Taylor about the journal a day or two before. It was careless of her, but I think it was her jealous anger that made her do it."

I thought of a question at this juncture, so asked, "Did you know where the book was hidden?"

"She didn't share that detail with me. I wasn't sure if the information had been beaten out of her by Taylor, so I followed him the better part of that night after chasing him out of the apartment in hopes that he would lead me to the book. When it was obvious that he wasn't going anywhere in particular, I returned to the apartment just in time to see you and the Inspector leaving. On a hunch, I followed the both of you to Santa Monica, and watched when you went into the carousel building. I'd remembered then that Betty Jean had an uncle who worked there and figured rightly that's where she left the book. You had found it. The only question was, were you holding onto it yourself, or did you pass it on to the police. I thought it might be the latter, but I had to be sure. That was why I came to your office the following night. You were playing it really cagey, so I couldn't be sure. Of course I already knew it wasn't in your office, I had searched it, but there was always the chance you were holding it somewhere else. It wasn't until I stumbled upon you while keeping an eye on Taylor at Grauman's Chinese Theater that I knew for certain that you'd given it to the police. Although, for a short moment, I did entertain the thought that you might have double crossed me and offered it to Taylor, but then as soon as I said it, I realized that you were too much of a 'straight shooter' to do so."

"Thanks. I think," I replied lamely.

"So, I realized then that I couldn't depend on my 'insurance policy' to protect me..."

"And that's when you really went on the offensive with Taylor," I finished for him.

He didn't answer, but I figured his silence confirmed it. One last question crossed my mind so I asked, "This is just a minor point, but you said you'd called the police and told them to go to Betty Jean's apartment. If you were so busy chasing Taylor that night, when did you find time to do so?"

"I told you, I chased him out of the apartment, but he thought he'd lost me. I followed him unobserved for the remainder of the evening. The first moment he stopped to rest, I found a phone booth and called."

Well, by this time my narrative had really gone afar field, and I hadn't even gotten to what I felt was the most important point; one that would reveal the real truth of this murder investigation!

23

FINAL ACT: A KILLER IS REVEALED

We all are guilty, at one time or another, of wearing masks. But most of these are donned innocently to disguise insecurities or hide self-perceived weaknesses. Not so with a killer. His mask is to disguise the face of a hideous monster; the leprous skin of a creature whose countenance plagues society. To the uninformed they're just a friend, neighbor, teacher, or politician, but when that mask slips and the true face is revealed, they're never looked at as human again.

" **I**f trouble comes in multiples, for Taylor it reached its potential with Miss Hyland. For one thing, he realized early on that she wasn't as cool and calculating as himself. My persistence in pursuing this investigation and constant scrutiny of her, concerned him. He wasn't sure she could hold up under the pressure. So he did everything he could either to discourage me off the case, like trying to drop a vase on my head," I looked directly at him at that point. "I realize that was you. Hard to prove, but it had to be. You must have overheard the secretary giving me instructions to the property department. You were in the next office for the staff meeting. It wouldn't take any stretch of the imagination that when she buzzed Clemmons, you realized I was in the office, excused yourself and found a convenient spot to eavesdrop on us without being seen. You then followed me to the property department, where you tried hitting me with the vase. In another instance, you took a potshot at me at the pool. I believe here you were trying to accomplish two things: again, to frighten me, but also to maintain the illusion of threat around Hyland and shift any suspicions I may've had regarding her. That's why the disguise again… to make it look like Rappo, or at least generate more confusion to upset any conclusions that I may've reached. Miss Hyland's reaction to the charade, however, tipped me off. She did her best to delay me investigating the shooting until you had time to get away.

"And then there was that little act you put on at the Santa Monica Pier. I have to admit that was the most creative of all. No doubt by this point you felt that I was getting close to the truth. You figured I had my hands on the black book and you weren't altogether sure just how far your former partners had gone to expose you in its pages. When Miss Hyland called you from Bullocks Wilshire, you'd rightly assumed that you were next on my list. You worked fast, doing something that normally you wouldn't have done unless your back was up against a wall, and that was to confide in another confederate; Soames in this instance. I'm not sure what you told him, perhaps that I had also learned his secret as well, or maybe you just openly blackmailed him. Whatever the case, you convinced him to dress up as Rappo and play along with that farce you put on for me at the pier. It might have been easier to have him murder me in the disguise of Rappo, but that was too risky to propose, especially if Soames turns out not to play along, so you came up with this seemingly harmless plan. A little smoke and mirrors using guns with blanks, and a bag filled with fake blood strapped under your shirt, no doubt courtesy of Champion's special effects department, and the illusion of your murder was complete… with Rappo once again being set up as the fall guy. The tumble over the railing and the swim was nothing for you. I checked up on your background. Aside from being a film editor at that studio in New Jersey, you started off doing stunts there, and you were also an excellent swimmer, having been a lifeguard for a couple of summers during your youth at Atlantic City. Of course, having someone else in on the scam did propose some dangers. He might talk. For you the solution was simple. Soames must've told you about the drug deal planned for that evening. You just passed the information anonymously over to Vice, and then waited at the Bowl with your shotgun to murder him in the confusion that was likely to occur during the execution of the police action."

"And how would being dead benefit Taylor in the long run?" Clemmons asked suddenly.

"For one, he could disappear, thereby giving him the freedom to try and dispose of me and any other witness like Adams, which could be a danger to him. He could then later return, perhaps citing amnesia for his absence… or he could simply change his identity and, to the world, remain dead."

"And his plan might have succeeded if he'd killed the both of ya up at Arrowhead," Red added.

"Agreed," I replied. "But let's return to where I left off regarding Miss Hyland. With all the reservations that Taylor may've had about her mental state, there was a physical one that could've put a monkey wrench in his plans. Vanity has its limits, but for Taylor it could well spell disaster for him. Nerve is important, especially behind a trigger, but so is good eyesight, which is something Miss Hyland didn't have. Vanity prevented her from wearing glasses… although she had them, but she didn't let on until… and here I'm guessing, just before the murder. Taylor was counting on Miss Hyland to take Geary out quickly with one shot and quite frankly learned late in the game that she couldn't hit the side of a barn door if it was placed directly in front of her."

"How do you know that?" Clemmons interrupted.

"When I was at her pool, she asked me who was approaching. It was her father. I said so. He was close enough for me to see him clearly, but not so for her. Then again on another visit, when she dropped her purse at the front of their estate… when I helped her pick up the contents, I spotted her glasses among the items spilled. I followed up yesterday by contacting her optometrist. He stated that she was 20/40. In other words, she suffers from myopia or near-sightedness."

"So, Taylor didn't use her to pull the trigger?" Clemmons asked. "I don't understand. You said earlier that she used the excuse of getting water to get her over to the area of the prop boxes. The area designated for the shooter?"

"Oh, she was there all right. She told me that herself, although she didn't realize it. She said that she saw Rappo pass her heading in the direction of the set. Rappo said it was while he was heading back to the set that the murder had occurred. If that was true, Hyland had to be in the area of the boxes during the time of the murder."

"So Hyland *did* commit the murder?" Clemmons asked. "I'm confused."

"In answer to that, I'd like to address this question to Miss Hyland," I turned to her. She was scared. I could see it. But I needed this question answered… and

I needed it answered truthfully. "Listen, this is important. How you answer this could mean the difference between going free or doing time. You must answer this in all honesty. As the good book says, 'the truth shall set you free.' Therefore... think very carefully before answering. Understand?" She nodded slowly. "Describe for me the gun you used to kill Geary."

She blinked, but after a long pause answered, "Medium size, black all over with a ring on the handle."

I turned to Red. "Based on your knowledge of weapons, what did she just describe?"

"A Webley," he answered simply.

"But Miss Geary was killed with a Smith and Wesson revolver. The bullet recovered from Geary's body was a .38. The Webley Holds a .455 caliber round. Therefore, she couldn't possibly have been the killer."

A buzz arose throughout the room. When it simmered down, Fran Adams was the first to speak:

"You've been all over the place, Logan. I'm really lost. If Hyland wasn't the killer then who was?"

"You were," I stated firmly.

Another moment passed as various gasps filled the room. "You're crazy, Logan," Adams protested. What makes you think I'm the killer? You're just trying to protect your client!"

"There are three very good reasons why I know that you're the killer," I said, raising my voice amongst the din and finally getting the crowd's attention. "For one, you had the motive and advantage. You were carrying an illegitimate child. Geary was blackmailing you for that, and Taylor was being set up for blackmail as well. Since he was your lover and the father of your child, you saw this as a double threat. I expect Taylor pointed this out to you as well. As for opportunity, you were over by the boxes. Rappo said he lost sight of you until after the murder…"

She started to protest again, but I continued, "Secondly, I did a little checking on your background. I heard you were quite an athlete in high school. It turns out that aside from archery and various other sports, you also won some medals for sharpshooting. That little display of fumbling with your father's shotgun didn't convince me…" She tried to interrupt, but I continued, "And the most damning of all…When we discussed it in the car you said that you couldn't handle a shotgun, let alone a revolver…*a revolver.* No one ever said that Geary was shot by a revolver…or even a pistol. It was being kept quiet by the police. The only person who knew was Soames, and he was sworn to silence…and when I double checked with him, he assured me that he had not told a soul. Therefore, there was only one way that you would have known *and that was if you shot her yourself!*"

She started to interrupt again, but I went on to explain quickly, "When Taylor realized that it was too risky to have Hyland as the trigger person due to her eyesight, he got you to play along. After all, you were a pistol champ. ..You wouldn't miss the target. Hyland was still put through the motions however, but purposely left in ignorance. Her gun was actually loaded with blanks, but she wasn't told that. For all intents and purposes, she was left to believe that she had actually killed Geary. However, when she pulled the trigger, it was you, who, having taken up position out of sight, somewhere behind her, simultaneously fired the lethal shot, and then afterwards left the gun on the bench in place of the one returned there by Hyland.

"Now, you may ask, why the deception? That's easy to answer. Hyland was made to believe she'd killed Geary, so Taylor once again had something to use as blackmail against her. Remember, he was no longer in possession of the nude photographs taken at Clemmons' party. And it would have worked, except that two things went wrong. Hyland had picked up and disposed of the wrong gun…"

"I didn't pull the trigger," Hyland suddenly interrupted. "I held up the gun and aimed, but I didn't pull the trigger. I panicked at the last moment and didn't follow through. It was a surprise when I saw that Geary had actually gotten shot. I never said anything because I felt no one would believe me."

"That's also true," I confirmed. "Because the gun Soames found had not been fired."

At this point I could see that Adams was angry, almost to the point of madness, and if it hadn't been for the audience I'm sure she would have lunged at me. I noticed the flush to her cheeks, and the wild stare in her eyes as she suggestively flexed her hands into claws. Taylor's reaction, on the other hand, was curious.

During the entire speech I kept glancing toward him and he seemed calm, almost to the point of amusement, a slight smile growing at the corner of his lips. When I'd finally concluded, he returned to his old applauding routine, and then stated, "Very good, Logan. I now realize that my biggest mistake was underestimating you. I thought you were just one dumb gumshoe, who I fooled once, and could do so again." He looked over at Adams. "Give it up, Fran, he's got us." She seemed stunned; his statement caught her totally by surprise. He turned to me again. "But, you got one thing wrong; it was never intended that Hyland take the blame. Do you think I'd cut off my gravy train?

"Hyland was too good an opportunity to waste," Taylor continued in a cold, matter-of-factly way. "I set her up for the reasons you mentioned, but I prepared a way out if something was to fail. She didn't pick up the wrong gun. She selected exactly the gun I set out for her. I also dropped the gun in the barrel for insurance in case something went wrong."

I have to admit that I was confused now, and must have shown it, because he went on further to explain, "It was always planned that Hyland would never commit the murder. I knew about her vision all along, after all we had been close friends…" I could see that this statement didn't sit well with Adams. He continued:

"Frannie and I had devised a plan whereby Hyland would think she committed the murder, but it was actually Frannie's keen eye that would pull off the killing. As you said, I needed something fresh on Hyland, something that would set me up for life. This was it. It would've come off perfectly except for that girl Williams and yourself. Betty Jean's presence on the set that day threw the whole plan. It was her comments that spurned you on; otherwise I believe you might have bought it."

Now it was my turn to ask a question. "You haven't explained about your insurance?"

"Simple," he replied smugly. "If someone saw her, or anything went wrong in that regard, I prepared those pieces of evidence to clear her."

"But that could have backfired," I added logically. "If Hyland was shown not to be guilty of the murder, then it would have to be someone else…"

"It wouldn't be me," he pointed out, "I had an alibi. As you recall, I was never away from the set and have witnesses who would swear to it."

"But what about Adams?" At the question he just smiled, and I instantly caught on. "You were planning to make Adams your sacrificial lamb." He nodded. "But, even at the cost that she might tell all?" He just smiled again, and it hit me. "But, it would never get that far, would it? She would meet with one of your accidents, or perhaps a staged suicide with a carefully forged confession note."

"You got it in aces, gumshoe," he replied with a thin, cruel smile.

"You cold hearted bastard!" Adams suddenly cried out. "How could you? I thought you loved me?"

"I told you I didn't want a kid," he responded coldly. "You could've done something about it. You knew it would just cramp my style."

"*Then it wasn't just Logan* you wanted to kill at Arrowhead," she replied. Either she had been in denial or the truth had finally dawned on her. "If your plans had worked out, you would've used that amnesia ploy to come back not to me, but to your precious Madeline. You'd be sitting pretty with her money, and I'd be lying with your child in a cold grave!"

An officer had been standing near her, and as she uttered that last statement she turned unexpectedly and removed his service revolver from its holster. Before anyone could stop her she took aim at Taylor and fired, hitting him squarely in the chest. The impact rocked him and the chair backwards onto the floor, where he lay dead. After a short struggle the gun was wrestled out of her hands and she was immediately taken into custody, and escorted out of the room with cuffs on her wrist.

A blanket was found for the body, and the assembly was promptly dismissed. However, once outside, Miss Hyland appeared quickly at my side. "I have to thank you, Logan," she began meekly. "I'm so sorry I had to lie to you in the beginning. It was just that he was so damn convincing. My mistake was to trust him." She paused thoughtfully, and then asked, "He was the person responsible for that second note sent to my house, wasn't he?"

"You'd asked him. What did he say?"

The response caught her by surprise.

"He said no, but how did you know?"

"It was you listening on the extension who overheard my call from Inspector Clancy," I stated simply. "That would explain how Taylor was able to trace Adams to Arrowhead so quickly. I don't think deep down she was really sure of him, or at least wanted to admit it to herself. He seemed surprised when I told him that she had disappeared, so I think it's safe to assume that she didn't leave word with him. In any case it was unexpected, and it could signal potential problems for him. That was why he needed to find her fast, and you provided that information."

"I didn't mean to exactly," she replied lamely. "He told me when I asked about the note that it was from Adams and that he needed to find her in order to protect me. I mean he was the only person I could turn to. The first note was his idea, and so naturally I would have questions about this second. I called him from work and then hurried home. When I got there I saw you had already arrived, so I went in the next room and listened in. When I heard you had a call from Inspector Clancy, I got onto the extension. After over-hearing that information on Adams' whereabouts, I called Taylor back with the information and he told me to delay you. But how did you know?"

"I take it you called from a different extension than the one you listened in on?" I asked.

"Yes. I thought I heard someone coming, so I had to change rooms quickly," she replied, still puzzled.

"Well, in your haste you must have forgotten to hang up the phone. It was discovered by your butler," I explained. "That's how I knew someone was listening on the line. Did you call Taylor from the garage?"

"Exactly," she replied. "I guess you figured that because I came running from the direction of the garage when I pretended to have just arrived. But, you still haven't answered my question. Was it Taylor or Adams who sent me that note?"

"It was Adams," I answered. "This was one of the few times that he was telling the truth. I remembered that the envelope I inspected at your home had a postmark from San Bernardino County. The letters on the note were the same as the first taken from the script, hence I figured she might have it still somewhere about the cabin. It was a long shot, granted… she could have gotten rid of it since… but it was worth a try. I had Inspector Clancy send some men to search… and it paid off. They found it hidden amongst some other books in the library. She was suspicious of Taylor's true relationship with you... actually to the point of jealousy. She didn't want to end up second banana, so that note was ordering you to back off. It was as simple as that."

24

EVERY END MUST HAVE A
NEW BEGINNING

Life always has a way of repeating itself. Just like the hands that circle the face of a clock. If it starts at twelve, it ends at twelve when it completes its full circumvention. People, places, and occurrences always seemed to come back to where they were in the beginning. There might be small variations from time to time, but ultimately, in the end, it always comes back to where it all began.

G uess you could call it Monday morning blues, or maybe it was just the letdown after coming off a case. The last couple of weeks had kept me occupied like a starving dog in a butcher shop, but now that was all over and I was again back to the old routine of waiting for the phone to ring or listening for the clatter of the elevator door in anticipation of a perspective client. As per my usual habit, I hung around the office until noon and then took the couple of blocks stroll along Hollywood Boulevard to my regular deli for my customary pastrami sandwich.

The marine layer had come in early that morning and decided to stay late; an unusual occurrence for that time of year. I think it was just a reflection of how I felt, or in any case, just amplified my moodiness.

I had just gotten my order and was taking a bite, sitting in my usual stool at the counter, when I felt a presence come up behind me, and from the scent of perfume didn't have to turn to tell it was a lady. A certain 'déjà vu,' if I could use such fancy French words came over me as I heard a voice whisper in my ear, "Logan…"

I turned half expecting to see Miss Hyland, but was greeted by Rita's sweet smile instead. Before I could answer, she explained, "Mattie told me that I could find you here." She jumped up onto the empty stool next to me.

"I was thinking of calling you," I began awkwardly. Which incidentally, wasn't a lie. I'd felt like I needed some company.

"Sure, I've heard that line before. What is it, Logan? Do I seem too eager? I mean, I always seem to scare men away."

"Eager wouldn't exactly be the word I would use. 'Forward,' even, a 'tease' might be a better description of it."

"You're being cruel." She pouted. I found it kind of cute.

"I really like you, Logan," she continued. "Do you think there might be a chance for us?"

I looked into her warm, emerald green eyes, and answered sincerely, "Sure kid, why not?" I have to admit I would've been crazy to answer otherwise. I then added, "And stop selling yourself short. You're a beautiful dame, with a lot of heart. A guy would count himself lucky to have you as his sweetheart."

"Then it's your lucky day," she replied with a broad smile.

I offered to buy her some lunch, but she declined. She said she would have to start beating the pavement looking for work.

"What happened with your job at the studio?" I think I knew the answer and didn't like it; still I had to ask.

"Clemmons fired me. He figured out that I snitched on him," I started to apologize, but she stopped me. "No, don't blame yourself. I should of known better… confidentiality and all. I'll be all right. Besides, he really wasn't that easy to work for. He had a big ego, with hands to match, if you know what I mean."

I still couldn't help feeling responsible. I wanted to help her, but was barely making it myself.

After I finished eating she asked to walk back with me to the office building. Partway, she took my hand. At first it seemed silly, like two kids walking home from school. But after some moments I starting thinking that it was kind of nice. As we reached the lobby I said good-bye, and she reached up and kissed me full on the lips. She was no school girl then, and I have to admit that I liked it even better. I was in the process of telling her that I would call her, when I sensed someone behind. He was trying to get my attention by tactfully clearing his throat, and when I turned I saw Alex, my mailman, looking rather uncomfortably at us both. He'd been de-livering the mail to the boxes in the lobby and I guess we were too preoccupied to note his presence.

"Excuse me," he said, handing over some enve-lopes. "I'm sorry to interrupt, Mr. Logan, but here's your mail."

"Thanks." I replied. I was thinking that it could've waited until I'd finished with the lady. After all, they were probably only bills and....

Suddenly an return address caught my attention. Rita started to walk off, but I called her back.

"What is it?" she asked.

"I don't know, but it's from Mr. Hyland of Hyland Dairy." I opened it quickly and read it, and then once again to believe it. I also took a long look at the check in the folds. One thousand dollars. I don't think I'd seen that much money in a long time, *and it was made out to me!*

Rita saw my expression, and asked again, "What is it?"

"It's a reception job for you and a car for me, and dinner… and dancing at the Coconut Grove for the both of us!" I said, unable to contain my exuberance as I swung her around. "It seems Daddy Hyland is appreciative for my efforts in clearing his daughter. He felt that the fifty dollars that she'd paid me wasn't nearly enough." At that point I showed her the check and she wrapped her arms around me and kissed me again. I'm sure Alex thought we were crazy but, hey, for that kind of dough, let him think what he wants.

The Coconut Grove was packed. It had been some time since I had seen so many "swells" in one room, and I was patting myself on the back as we walked in that I'd the forethought to rent a tux for the night. Rita was a knockout in her black evening gown, simply cut, yet stunning with her figure. She turned a few heads that evening. The Coconut Grove was a nightclub located at the Ambassador Hotel on Wilshire, a real first-class establishment that opened its doors nine years ago on New Year's Day, 1921.

A formally attired maitre d' placed us at a small round table covered by a white linen tablecloth, upon which sat a silver vase of delicate flowers, and a single shaded lamp. Music was coming from the elevated stage in the back of the room. A trio called the Rhythm Boys was performing with the Gus Arnheim Band, and one standout performer named Crosby was crooning a melodious tune. A large crowd was on the dance floor swaying in time to the music, while others sat at tables either talking or enjoying the excellent gourmet cuisine that was either being bussed out on carts or carried precariously on silver trays by tailed waiters from the kitchen. A seductively dressed cigarette girl in a flowered sarong, complete with lei, came over and asked if we needed anything, and another young lady with a camera snapped our picture.

"This is real class," I began awkwardly, glancing around. Scores of palms were placed about the room creating the illusion of a grove and hence the name.

The music stopped and a Master of Ceremonies drew up to the large square microphone on a tall stand. He introduced the celebrities in the audience that night: Gary Cooper, Jack Oakie, Will Rogers, and their dates. Needless to say necks were straining, but I was content keeping my eyes on Rita.

"What a beautiful silver setting," Rita exclaimed, carefully running her fingers along the utensils, which were placed next to a large china dinner plate and crystal water goblet. "I don't think I'll ever be able to afford something so nice."

A waiter brought us the menu, and I noticed Rita swallow hard when she saw the prices.

"Hey, don't worry about the cost… order whatever you want." I then reminded her, "It's on Hyland Dairies. And besides, it's a special occasion."

"What occasion is that?" she asked, looking quizzically over her menu.

"I have a proposal to make." The minute I uttered it, I realized I should've worded it differently. "How would you like a job as my receptionist?"

"No. I don't believe it!"

I started to stutter a protest, but stopped midsentence when I'd realized that it wasn't to my question that she was reacting, but to something that had just occurred behind me. I followed her stare over my shoulder and saw that our benefactors, the Hylands had just coincidentally walked in. Mr. Hyland was dressed meticulously in a well-tailored tuxedo and his daughter in the attractive, cobalt blue evening gown I'd seen on the model at Bullocks Wilshire. I think Rita's response had more to do with Mattie's appearance… you know, one of those things that happens when there are two hens and only one rooster in the hen house.

"I should invite them over," I reasoned.

"Do you have to, Tom?" she pleaded. "I was hoping we could be alone."

"So did I," I replied. "But after all they're the reason why we're here, and I don't think it would be polite to ignore them."

She reluctantly agreed, but not without a fair amount of pouting, and I walked over immediately to greet them. They were surprised at seeing me and graciously accepted my invitation.

"We didn't mean to interrupt your dinner," Mr. Hyland apologized as a waiter brought over two extra chairs. "We were just on our way home from a banquet at the Ambassador, and decided to see what was going on in the club. We don't plan to stay long."

I could see the relief in Rita's eyes. Luckily, I don't think the others noticed. The waiter came over and took our orders.

"My, Logan," Mattie said, leaning over and straightening my bow tie, "I've never seen you in anything other than your suit. You look real handsome in that tux tonight."

I felt Rita kick me under the table, and it took all my resistance not to wince at the sudden pain.

I turned to Mr. Hyland. "I want to thank you for your generous …"

"No, we have to thank you," Mr. Hyland interrupted, raising a hand. "If it wasn't for you, Mattie might have wrongly ended up in prison."

"Or worse," Mattie interjected, "tied up with that snake, Taylor!"

"I think he had big plans for you," I commented.

"You mean for my money," she corrected. "Taylor had only two loves: himself and cash. I realize that now. But you have to admit, he could be a charmer when it suited him."

"Yeah, charming," I added cynically. "He'd use anyone and anything that crossed his path. And he'd do so without remorse. Nice guy."

Why was it that women always fell for the wrong men? Was it their slick talk, or the danger they seemed to exude when they walked into a room? Did this aura awaken some sort of excitement in them? I guess that's one mystery I'll never solve.

"I believe Adams was right, if he'd killed you and Adams as he'd planned," Mattie continued, "the path would have been clear for him to return to me, feigning amnesia as an excuse for his absence. Who knows, maybe he had grand plans for marriage or, if not, use what he had on me for perpetual blackmail. Whatever the case, I'm so grateful that you saved me from him."

As Miss Hyland was expressing this, her gaze reflected sincere, heartfelt emotion. When she'd finished, she did so with her most candid smile.

"So what line did Taylor use to seduce you into killing Geary?" Rita asked. She said it innocently enough, but the quick glance she gave me spoke otherwise.

"Logan got it right earlier," she went on to explain. If she had noticed Rita's cattiness, she was playing the lady and ignoring it. "Taylor told me that he discovered that Geary and her friend with the scarf were the blackmailers and that my only solution was to carry out his plan. If I chose to go to the police, he was very adamant in his arguments that my secret would become public. He really painted a bleak picture. It left me no choice."

"I take it he never mentioned Geary's friend by name?" I asked and she nodded. "I thought so. He couldn't chance Rappo being identified; otherwise a connection might be made back to himself. Which was exactly what ultimately happened, but in a way he hadn't expected. It was, quite honestly, the turning point of the case."

We were all silent for a few minutes while the waiter brought both our entrees, and then Miss Hyland spoke up.

"Actually, Logan, it was fortunate we stumbled on to you tonight. We'd planned to look you up later." I raised an eyebrow and she continued, "I've decided to leave the movie industry, and Dad offered me a position with the dairy in management. It's quite a responsibility. I can't think of a woman today performing a job like this, but then again, Dad always was a risk taker." She nudged her father and he laughed.

"In any case, I could use some help," she continued, "and seeing that you once said if it was anything short of murder you might be interested...so what do you say? Are you interested in working for Hyland Dairies?"

It was tempting, at least for the briefest of moments, but I looked over at Rita and could see a sudden sadness cross her face. To make matters worse, Mattie added as a further incentive: "Think, Logan. It would give us a chance to get to know each other better."

"Thank you," I began slowly, and then looked over at Mr. Hyland. "Thank you both. But I've been in law enforcement all my life, and think I'd like to stick with it. Besides, I've gotten kind of used to being my own boss, and having to report to someone each day really doesn't have the appeal it used to." I then added quickly, "No matter how attractive they might be." She smiled at my compliment, and it accomplished what I had hoped for, to soften the blow. I wasn't brave enough to glance in Rita's direction.

"Well, very well," she said rising. "But the offer still stands in case you change your mind."

Her father took her cue and, after exchanging our final pleasantries, they disappeared through the exit.

"You sure, you wouldn't want to change your mind?" Rita asked after a long uncomfortable silence. She was staring down at her fork as she forlornly played with her vegetables. "I'm mean, it sounds like a good job, and…"

"She's not my type," I interrupted.

"What?" she asked, looking up quickly.

"I said she is not my type," I said smiling.

"But, she is beautiful and has loads of money."

"*I said she's not my type!*" I repeated with emphasis.

"Then what is your type?" she asked, her expression starting to brighten.

"How about looking in the mirror, kid," I stated simply, and then taking on a more business-like tone asked, "Now what about your answer. Are you interested in my job offer or not?"

She looked lovingly at me for a moment and then replied, *"Well, if it is anything short of murder I might be interested."*

THE END

Made in the USA
Monee, IL
09 November 2021